THE
MARINER'S
CURSE

JOHN LUNN

THE MARINER'S CURSE

To the
Ruth E. Dickenson
Library

Tundra Books

Published in Canada by Tundra Books,
481 University Avenue, Toronto, Ontario M5G 2E9

Published in the United States by Tundra Books of Northern New York,
P.O. Box 1030, Plattsburgh, New York 12901

Library of Congress Control Number: 2003112018

National Library of Canada Cataloguing in Publication

Lunn, John, 1958-
The mariner's curse / John Lunn.

For children aged 9-12.
ISBN 0-88776-672-2

I. Title.

PS8573.U57M37 2004   jC813'.6   C2003-905208-7

We acknowledge the financial support of the Government of Canada
through the Book Publishing Industry Development Program (BDIDP)
and that of the Government of Ontario through the Ontario Media
Development Corporation's Ontario Book Initiative. We further
acknowledge the support of the Canada Council for the Arts and the
Ontario Arts Council for our publishing program.

This is a work of fiction and any resemblance of characters
to persons living or dead is purely coincidental.

Design: Cindy Reichle

Printed and bound in Canada

This book is printed on acid-free paper that is 100% recycled,
ancient-forest friendly (40% post-consumer recycled).

1 2 3 4 5 6   09 08 07 06 05 04

To my wife, Meredith, for her everlasting
encouragement and support of my dreams

Acknowledgments

I would like to thank the following people for all their help in bringing this book to life: Yvonne Coleman, Cindy Davis, Ann Hoey, Robin Lunn, Bob and Martha Naylor, David Strugnell, and Andrea Thorpe for taking time to read and advise; all my young readers – Ben Naylor and Alissa, Ariel, and Garrett Hubert; Kathy Lowinger and Sue Tate at Tundra for their meticulous and insightful editing; my agent, Leona Trainer, at TLA; and, especially, my mother and lifelong editor, Janet Lunn, for countless hours and guidance through all the years that have made me a better writer.

Contents

Rory Goes to Sea

Aboard at last! Standing on the deck of a sea bound ship is where I belong, Rory Dugan sighed happily. It didn't matter that the *Sea Lion* was an ocean liner, and not a clipper or destroyer. Nor did it matter that he was a twelve-year-old boy wandering around the main lobby, and not a hearty sailor high in the rigging of the mizzenmast. All that mattered was that he was going to sea. Crossing the Atlantic Ocean from Southampton to New York.

The enormous lobby was busier than a subway station at rush hour, and Rory had already lost his mother in the crowd. This was the fanciest place he'd ever seen. All dark wood walls with brass trim, plush green carpeting, and brown leather furniture. It was open in the middle, like a shopping mall with a dazzling spiral staircase – brass rails gleaming and thick glass steps leading up to two other levels.

He usually had no trouble spotting his mother because of her bright red hair. But being short didn't help in this crowd. He squeezed through a noisy mob of bustling passengers, porters with luggage, and busy waiters. *Maybe I can go upstairs and look over the railing for her,* he thought. He looked way up at the balconies and tried to figure out where would be a good perch. He could see a –

"*Oooof!*" Something hit him and drove the air from his lungs like a popped tire. He clutched his chest in pain, crumpled up, and hit the floor, his new glasses spinning across the carpet.

Someone asked, "Are you alright?"

"He came out of nowhere," said another.

Rory looked up at a wash of blurry faces as he fumbled around for his glasses. *If I lose those ugly things, Mom will kill me* was the first desperate thought he had. His fingers found the lenses and he planted the glasses back on his nose. Things got worse. He was woozy and wondered if this was his first attack of seasickness. It sure wasn't what he expected. He smiled helplessly at the distorted faces around him.

"Give me those!" a man's angry voice growled.

Before Rory could think, the glasses were snatched off his face and another pair were thrust into his hands. He put them on and the world refocused. Sprawled on the floor beside him was a very old man, with a spotty weathered face full of wrinkles and bushy gray whiskers, attaching the other glasses to his own bony nose. He had the stub of a cigar clenched between crooked yellow teeth and froze Rory with a glare that could raise warts.

Rory dropped his eyes, half embarrassed and half scared. He didn't know where the old guy could have come from so fast. *I must have run right into him,* he figured. A couple of men reached down and put their hands under the old man's elbows to hoist him to his feet.

"Let me be!" he roared, with a voice like a ripsaw, and yanked his arms away so fiercely he nearly toppled over again. "You think me frail? Why, you pups, I'll dance on your graves!"

The two men backed away, holding their hands up. "Suit yourself, pops," said one.

"That boy ran right into you!" said a woman in pink tights. "I saw the whole thing."

Rory's mother, Claire Farentino, appeared through the thicket of onlookers and helped him up. "What happened, Rory? What's going on?" She was a tiny woman, who looked like a wind could blow her over. With her dyed red hair, sparkling eyes, and sharp features, he sometimes thought she looked like an exotic bird.

"I'm sorry. I didn't see –" Rory began.

"That's plain enough!" snapped the old man. He plucked the cigar from his teeth, and his eyes darted here and there as though he wasn't sure where he was. "The child should be on a leash, madam," he said, recovering himself. He brushed off his jacket sleeves and straightened his cuffs. Reaching down, he scooped up his brown felt hat with a gnarled old hand. "First he capsizes me, then tries to snatch my spectacles."

"Rory? Why would he want your glasses?" Claire asked him, baffled.

Rory didn't dare speak. He stole a guilty glance at the disapproving faces of the strangers gathered around. It didn't look good. *Old man: 10, Rory: 0.*

"The boy is dangerous," an elderly woman declared, clicking her teeth. "If it was me, I'd have broken a hip for sure."

"I'm sorry, sir. Are you hurt?" Claire asked the old man while she brushed him off, as if to help smooth his hackles.

"No, madam. I am not," his buzz saw voice replied. He slapped the hat on his head and snatched a walking stick that someone held out to him. Then he shot Rory another vile stare. As their eyes met, Rory froze. A lump slithered down his throat like an ice snake and wrapped a coil of cold fear around his heart. He couldn't tear his eyes away.

For an instant, Rory found himself back in the past, standing beside that pool, helplessly watching his brother, Ian, thrash around and gasp for air. It felt like a hand had gripped his throat and was squeezing this horrible memory from him. Then it released him and he reeled back, as though he'd just been slapped.

"Lay off my course, boy!" the old man warned, and limped off through the crowd.

After a stunned silence, Rory's mom looked at him. "What was that all about? You went sheet white," she said. The few remaining bystanders whispered reproachfully, then went off about their business.

Rory could barely find his voice. "I did . . . I mean, I didn't. . . ." He stopped. His eyes were riveted on the spot where the old man had stood. "I didn't see him," he finally said. The stabbing, painful image of Ian vanished so fast, he wasn't sure it had happened.

"Oh, well. You might try to be more careful," his mom scolded.

"Uh-huh," he agreed absently. He shouldered his duffel bag and shuffled after her across the lobby to the elevators, trying to figure out what just happened. Rory's new stepfather, Eddie Farentino, was waiting for them with the rest of the luggage.

"What's going on?" he asked.

"Rory ran some poor old man down," Claire explained. "Honestly, Rory, you should pay more attention."

"Typical," Eddie added.

Rory couldn't stand Eddie. With his flabby gut tucked into a BIG EDDIE'S DEALS ON WHEELS T-shirt, he acted like a big cheese because he owned a couple of used-car lots. Rory thought he was a know-it-all jerk, like one of those greasy fatsoes who play a gangster's bodyguard in the movies. Guys that are always nicknamed things like Poundcake or Meatball. *The less said about Eddie, the better,* he thought.

"That old man was totally weird," Rory whispered to his mother as they all rode the crowded glass elevator up. "Do you think he's a wacko?"

"What do you expect when you knock people down all over the place?" she replied. "He's probably a perfectly nice man who thinks you're the one who's a wacko."

Rory didn't disagree. All the same, he felt there was something deeply creepy about the old man. Something decidedly not right. He rubbed his chest where they'd collided, then turned to more pleasant thoughts. . . .

This was the first time he'd ever been at sea, even though he had been in love with ships, especially the *Titanic,* for years. He'd read books about them, drawn up blueprints, and built models of them. He had wanted to take this trip so badly that he'd promised to do anything his mom asked. Even get good grades and behave during the boring week they had just spent in England.

Eddie poked a chubby finger into his ribs. "Wait'll you see the great cabin we got, sport," he crowed, as people got off on Deck 1.

Rory flinched and swiped at the finger. "It's called a stateroom. And stop calling me sport."

"Whatever," Eddie replied.

Right outside the elevator doors, a waterfall splashed over pink stones. Surrounding it were a few small trees and vines, with a sweet musty scent that wafted into Rory's nose. Overhead a skylight cast glimmers of afternoon light through the leaves that glinted like diamonds on the splashing water. *Wow!* Rory thought all it needed was a parrot or a monkey to be like a real jungle. It sure wasn't like any ship he'd ever imagined. Still in the elevator, they all three stood with mouths gaping.

"Are we staying *here*?" Rory asked, as Eddie stopped the door from closing on them.

"Isn't it magical?" Claire said and wrapped her tiny hands around Eddie's arm. She filled her lungs with the musty perfume. "I can't wait to see our stateroom," she added, with a wink at Rory.

"Grab those bags, sport," Eddie told Rory and jammed some luggage in the door. "What's the room number, hon?"

Claire fumbled in her purse and plucked the tickets out. "*Oops*. Deck 11, cabin 40. This is the wrong deck. It says 1, not 11."

"On a ship, the low numbers always start at the top," Rory explained.

With a heavy sigh, Eddie dragged the bags back in and pressed 11. "Betcha it'll be just as nice," he said, as they started down.

Picking up and letting off other passengers all the way down, they finally got to 11 – the bottom passenger deck. It could have been on another planet it was so different from the waterfall jungle. They peered through the elevator doors down a long narrow passage with overhead pipes. It was painted all white, with blue carpeting and a wooden handrail along both walls that was broken only by the bright blue cabin doors. As they dragged the bags out, they caught a whiff of stuffy air mixed with the smell of a cafeteria. It reminded Rory of the crappy lunches served at his school. This was more what he expected, even if it was a letdown.

Eddie rolled along cheerfully, keeping an eye on the door numbers as they hauled their luggage down endless corridors and squeezed past other passengers moving in to the cabins. They passed the doors to the main kitchen, where the reek of industrial-strength cooking hit hardest.

"Here we are," Eddie grunted. "Number 1140." He swiped the key card in the slot to unlock the door. "*TA DA!* Home for the week."

Rory plunged in first. The room seemed no wider than the hallway, with a tiny round window at the far end. There was a sofa and dresser with a TV and a huge mirror behind it and a double bed under the window. A curtain could be drawn between the sofa and the bed. Besides a phone-booth-sized bathroom next to the door, that was it. He figured his bedroom at home was bigger than the whole works. To top it off, the reek of the kitchen hung in the air.

Claire crinkled her nose. "Oh, Eddie. Are you sure?" She heaved her suitcase onto the bed, crossed her arms, and gave the room a cold once-over. "It's awful small for three of us, don't you think, honey?"

Eddie shrugged and closed the door. His beefy body cut the room in half. "It's meant to be cozy. And we didn't expect to have Rory with us. Anyways, how much time we gonna stay here when there's so much action on board? Like food. That kitchen smell is making me hungry."

"It's called a galley," Rory informed him and pushed his glasses up his nose.

"My mistake," Eddie replied, throwing up his hands.

Rory pressed his face to the window. They were practically at sea level. Tugboats chugged around the harbor between huge ships, all blowing stacks of black smoke into the sky while going about their business. Up close, the water was brown and almost splashed against their window. In the reflection of the glass, he watched Eddie the Poundcake wrap his big mitts around Mom. *Any second they will go into their smooching routine. Yuck. I guess I should expect it. After all, this is their honeymoon.*

He recalled his real dad's phone call before they had left home. Rory couldn't go to Chicago for vacation because Dad suddenly had to go away on business. So Eddie and Mom agreed to take him to England with them. He had wanted to come for the boat trip, but the past week of boring hotels, museums, and icky restaurants had been agony. He'd felt like one of the suitcases the whole time.

Mom had met Eddie when she was looking for a new car. That was six months ago. Since then everything was Eddie, Eddie, Eddie. Now that they were married and he was moving in with them, things would only get worse. *What a drag. . . .*

Rory wished life was like it was when his dad lived at home. That was years ago. Before . . . the accident. He hated thinking about it because he always felt it was his fault. But he was only eight at the time and Ian was six. They were left alone for a second. Long enough for Ian to jump into the deep end of the pool after a toy. Ian couldn't swim and Rory couldn't save him. By the time his mom came back, it was too late: Ian was gone. It tore their family apart. Rory withdrew into himself; Mom and Dad started to fight all the time. A year later, Dad moved out. Rory knew deep inside it was all his fault, even though his parents and all those counselors said different. He knew the truth. He was in charge and Ian had died.

Funny, he thought, as he flopped on the tiny sofa, *I haven't thought about Ian for a long time.* Just thinking about him always made his gut hurt. The easiest way to cope was to be invisible. So that's what he did. He lived in his dreams and the world of ships.

"Guess this is my berth," he mumbled. He unpacked his gear, carefully selecting places for everything. He put his laptop and mini printer at one end; his software, comic books, and CDs at the other; and dropped all his clothes in a heap on the floor.

"Pick 'em up there, sport," Eddie ordered, almost before they landed.

An hour later, the *Sea Lion* set sail. Rory had dreamed of this moment a thousand times, but reality was way better than anything he could imagine. He could hardly feel the ship move, it was so smooth. As he leaned over the railing and looked down the shiny blue steel hull to the tiny people on the dock far below, it looked as though the dock was moving and they were stationary. Streamers and confetti showered over everyone like falling snow. Cheers and shouts from ship and shore alike, along with blasts from the ship's horn, ushered the floating city away from the dock.

Nothing had prepared Rory for the unbelievable size of this ship. He had seen photos in the brochure and imagined being on the *Titanic*, but pictures couldn't show the enormity. He had read that the ship was bigger than three football fields and that it weighed 100,000 tons. But those were just numbers and hard to picture. This was a skyscraper! It was as big as the Empire State Building floating on its side. Not only that, over three thousand people would be living aboard for the next week. They would be separated from the world, like explorers or astronauts. That notion sent a thrill right through him. A thrill of both excitement and fear.

Once they were launched and had attended a safety drill at their muster station, Rory took the elevator straight to Deck 5, where there was a foredeck at the bow. It was a big open area, with a steel floor and a railing around the rim like the front of a ferryboat. He wanted to stand there as the ship navigated the English Channel. A small crowd of people with the same idea were already there.

Elbows on the railing, with seagulls wheeling and screaming overhead, he watched the land slip past as the ship made her way through calm water. It was a warm afternoon and the air smelled heavily of fish and the oily harbor. With the wind in his face and the ship carving a road through the sea, Rory couldn't imagine a better place to be. Off the starboard bow, the hilly coastline of England – partially shrouded in mist – faded to the blue of the sky above and the sea below. There were other ships in the lanes: tankers, sailboats, and cargo ships, all making their way to and from Europe. They looked like toys from where he stood. He knew that this was the view the passengers on the *Titanic* had had as she left England in April 1912.

Living in Kansas, Rory had never spent time near water. He loved the idea of the quiet open space of the ocean much more than the open skies of the prairies because the thought of being unreachable at sea appealed to him. However, under his sandy bangs, which only ever got combed with his fingers, and blue eyes squinting through a first pair of glasses that itched his ears, he knew he looked more like a boy from the world of computers than a suntanned seaman.

He thought everything about himself was gawky and stupid, and never liked looking in a mirror. Still under five feet, he was a bit short for twelve. He was all elbows and knees, tripping into things. His nose and chin were pointy like his mother's, but his ears stuck out like his dad's. Add in the geeky wire glasses and he figured he was the goofiest-looking kid in school.

Since Ian's death, Rory had withdrawn from his friends and family. At school he ate alone and spent his free time at the computers, or in the library. At home he read stories, watched movies, and explored the Internet for chat groups and other stuff on ships. His attitude came off as snobby to the boys at school. They teased him and called him Retard Rory. It didn't help that he tried to use a vocabulary that he could barely manage.

Rory took off his glasses to wipe away the sea mist. The memory of getting them knocked off by the strange old man made him queasy, like suddenly recalling forgotten homework just before school. Everything about the old guy was so weird. Those crooked teeth, hollow eyes, and spotty bald head. He was almost like a skeleton in that old-fashioned tweedy suit and tie. He had one of those high white collars and buttoned vests you see in old movies. In fact, he was so out of place with everyone else in their sports clothes and T-shirts, it was like he had been dropped on the ship from some other time.

But it was the poisonous stare and strange words that creeped Rory out most. The expression, "I'll dance on your graves," had him really spooked. Like that nasty sensation you get when you hear a noise behind you when you're walking home alone at night. You don't want to turn around because you don't really want to know if someone is there, but you've got to find out for sure. Strangely, the more he thought about the incident, the less detail he remembered.

Rory shuddered and looked over his shoulder to see if anyone noticed. He was alone! All the other passengers had left the foredeck without him even noticing. The ship was headed for open sea and his grumbling stomach told him it was probably time for supper.

A Suspicious Character

Early the next morning, Rory was bursting to get out and explore every corner of the ship. As fast as he could, he stuffed down the bagel and cream cheese his mom had ordered with coffee and was ready to bolt by eight o'clock. He put on his favorite white shirt with blue piping, blue jeans, and white sneakers. He thought he looked great. Like a real sailor.

Snatching his mother's room key, he shouted, "I promise I'll check in for lunch!" and shot out the door. *This is great!* he thought. *Lots to do and no one to bug me all day.* He would start at the top with the bridge and navigation systems. From there, he would work his way down towards the engines.

Sea Lion had a total of fifteen decks, each one the size of a shopping mall. The top three had two pools, a climbing wall, tennis, minigolf, and a bunch of pubs and discos. The bridge and officers' quarters were there as well. Below that were two decks of luxury staterooms, a gymnasium, and a casino. Decks 6, 7, and 8 had the main dining room, shops, the promenade, theaters, and too much other stuff to even remember. On Decks 9 to 11 were hundreds of standard staterooms crammed together, the main kitchens, and the lobby. Below Deck 11 were all the crew cabins, engine operations, and fuel tanks. Those decks were off-limits to passengers.

After about an hour, he realized it wasn't going to be easy to get to the places he wanted. He was back on the foredeck on Deck 5, dangling his legs over the side between the rails, looking at the sea roll under the bow far below his feet. That morning the deck was deserted and the air smelled cleaner than it had the day before. *For a hotel,* Rory thought, *the ship is nice. For a hotel.* Everywhere was sparkling with glass, polished brass, and wood. All floors in the cabins, hallways, and common rooms were either carpeted or hardwood. There were over a thousand crew members on board to run the ship and look after the two thousand passengers. There were a lot of doors marked PRIVATE. He didn't have the guts to go through those. At least, not yet.

But that's where he wanted to go. The hotel part was boring. He wanted oval doorways with watertight wheel cranks, and cramped control rooms with lots of equipment and those neat lightbulbs in cages.

At least sitting there looking down at the waves made him feel like a sailor. He scouted the horizon for pirate ships, imagining himself aboard the *Hispaniola* with Jim Hawkins, on their way to Treasure Island. Sunshine glinted off the crests of the rippling waves and warmed his face and hands. He dropped a wad of paper overboard and counted the seconds it took to reach the water. Four. It was a long way down. He pushed his glasses up to make sure they didn't plummet to the same fate.

He remembered going with his dad to pick out the gold wire frames almost a year earlier. Dad had said they were cool. Rory had never worn glasses and thought every pair was ugly. But he was amazed at the difference in his vision with them on. He trusted his dad, so he picked these. He didn't know why, but he could talk to Dad in ways that he couldn't anymore with Mom. He could talk to him and tell him stuff like he was afraid of water, even though he felt stupid saying it. Maybe because Dad didn't always have an answer, or didn't try to protect him from bad thoughts the way Mom did. She constantly wanted to say something to make him feel better, even if she couldn't. Dad just listened and sometimes told him about things that he remembered when he was a kid.

An old couple came out on the deck. Their conversation broke in on Rory's thoughts. He looked around at them and noticed the door marked PERSONNEL ONLY, next to the stairs. The way to the rooms he wanted to see most was right through that door. His eyes moved up to the huge row of windows that spanned the entire width of the ship only four decks above. That was the bridge. From there the captain had a similar view to the one in front of Rory. But the captain was in command of the ship and that made all the difference in the world. *I could go on one of the tours,* he reminded himself, *but right now I want to find things on my own. This is vexatious.* He liked the fancy word for difficult.

Rory got up and meandered down the port side, looking in polished windows and clanging up and down freshly painted stairs between decks. There were a lot of people up now and not many places to be alone. On the top deck he saw a large group of kids playing games with a staff woman near the climbing wall and decided to avoid them altogether.

He took the first set of stairs down and kept going to make sure he was well out of reach. He stopped on Deck 7 to look at the lifeboats. There was a row of doors along each side of the ship that led out to the boats, which hung on hooks overhead. Numbered supply rooms at the muster stations just opposite the boats held all the safety gear and life jackets. His muster number was fifteen. If there was an emergency, he was supposed to report there. A few people were admiring the size of the lifeboats and taking pictures of each other standing under them. Rory watched for a while and then peeked into the windows of the supply rooms. The rooms were narrow and full of metal shelves and hooks, all bulging with gear. Rory noticed someone moving around inside one and he took a closer look.

It's that old man! He was rooting through some safety equipment and writing things on a notepad. Rory ducked below the window and slowly raised his head again to peer through the glass. *It's him alright: the same old tweed suit, bushy gray whiskers, and tiny glasses bobbing around on the end of his beaky nose.* Strangely, with the brown felt hat and gold-capped walking stick, the old man didn't look out of place in the suit. It just didn't fit on the ship. The old man's glasses caught the light and reflected two bright disks into Rory's eyes. He ducked down again and crouched on his haunches, wondering what to do next. He didn't remember the chilling fear that the old man had pricked him with the day before. Right now all he felt was curiosity.

What is he doing in here? Rory wondered. *Is he a spy or a crook?* He heard the door click and the old man shuffled out into the passageway. Rory looked at his sneakers and drummed his fingers on the side of his head to hide his face. Uneven footsteps slowly clumped away. He peeked through his fingers to see the old man limping off down the deck, supported by his walking stick. As soon as he rounded a corner at the end of the muster stations, Rory jumped up and followed. The scene reminded him of a James Bond movie, where Bond followed a Spectre agent around a submarine. He decided the old guy was on a secret mission. Rory code-named him Seadog.

He tailed Seadog from a distance, watching him poke around in bins, tap on windows, and write things on his pad. By a slow and winding route, the old man led the way down several decks to the main galley, near Rory's cabin on Deck 11. Rory could smell something baking all the way down the hall. Seadog disappeared through the galley door marked PRIVATE. Rory scrunched his fists tight. *Rats. Come on, you can do it, too. What's the worst that can happen? They'll throw you out? This is no time to be timid.* "After all, it's a matter of national security, Mr. Bond," he muttered.

His ears picked up a sound from around the corner that was worse than fingernails on a blackboard. Eddie. "I assumed you put my key in your purse, that's all," he was saying. Rory could tell he was mad. And getting closer.

"Now, Eddie, I'd forgotten that he took the other key," he heard his mom reply.

"Yeah. But now we have to find the squirt to let us back in," Eddie grumbled.

"The purser can make us a copy," she said, and Rory thought he could hear a note of impatience in her voice, too.

That does it. Better hauled off to the brig for trespassing than help Eddie out. Rory put his palms to the door and pushed his way into the galley. He was instantly transported to a world of rattling pots, people shouting, and a thousand smells that seemed much nicer here than out in the hall. The whole place was shiny stainless steel: the walls, floor, counters, shelves, doors, everything! All the cooks were wearing white, with tall hats, giving orders to waiters in black tuxedos. He didn't see Seadog, but with people kneading bread and chopping up meat and veggies, it was hard to tell who was there. In all that confusion no one noticed him wandering around. They just whipped past him as though he were part of the furniture.

Well, almost no one.

"Hey, kid," someone said close to his ear. His heart skipped. Slowly, he turned his head. A young waiter loading a cart with desserts was smiling at him.

Rory let out a relieved breath. He smiled back.

"You gonna get run over, you stand still like that," the waiter said, waving him closer. He was wearing a black jacket and red bow tie. He didn't look any older than the high school kids Rory knew. "You want a chocolate?"

"Sure."

The waiter handed Rory a big pastry on a doily. Rory shoved it all in his mouth, and then remembered to say thank you. It came out *"hooank-oo."* The pastry melted like buttery chocolate heaven. Instantly he liked this guy and looked hopefully at the cart of goodies.

"You like the galley better than the pool, maybe?" the waiter asked and flashed a very bright smile. He had a foreign accent. *Spanish,* Rory thought.

"I was looking around," Rory said guiltily, his mouth still full.

"S'okay. I am not telling you to leave."

"Thanks." Rory swallowed the rest quickly. "Did you see an old guy come in here a couple of minutes ago?"

"You mean that old corpse?"

"Yeah, I guess."

"He's yelling at Anatole through there." He pointed to a door on the other side of the room. Then he knuckled Rory's hair and gave him another pastry. "Gotta go, my friend. See you around." He pushed the cart away.

"Thanks," Rory said again. He crammed the second treat into his mouth in one bite as well. This one was a raspberry chocolate something and he couldn't close his mouth once he'd stuffed it in. He made a mental note to come back to the galley. *This is alright. . . .*

Cheeks bulging as he tried to chew, Rory shifted his eyes to the door the waiter had pointed to and pushed through into another busy part of the kitchen. He spotted the old man leaning on his walking stick, arguing with a chef in a soiled white smock who was waving a ladle in the air. Through all the crashing plates and loud voices, Rory couldn't hear what they were saying, but it didn't look like they liked each other. Finally, the chef stabbed his ladle at Seadog, who swatted at it and then limped away through another door. Rory followed.

He found himself back in the same quiet passage, staring down a row of blue doors. *This is just a big circle,* he thought, *except Eddie is gone.* He waited until Seadog disappeared around a corner before creeping up and peeking around. The old man had stopped in the middle of a passage between two cabins. Rory withdrew and then took another peek, just in time to see him step right through the wall and disappear!

"What?" he cried. "How did you do that!?" He ran up to the spot and pushed on the wall. It was solid. There was no door. There were cabin doors on either side, but Rory was sure that the old guy hadn't been standing there. He ran his fingers gingerly across the surface and probed the door frames. He found nothing except the railing. *Nothing!* He pulled and pushed on the rail, but it didn't budge.

Can he just disappear? Did he vanish like a ghost? Rory backed away and stared. *Maybe cruise ships can be haunted like houses and castles. Nah. There has to be a trick.* He had another go at the wall. Starting up as high as he could reach, he ran his hands around the entire edge between the two cabin doors. There wasn't anything. The wall was smooth as paper all the way down.

Suddenly, one of the doors jerked open. A lady in T-shirt and curlers stood there. "What do you want, kid?" she demanded, a cigarette drooping from the corner of her mouth.

"*Uh.*" Rory's mouth fell open. "Sorry, I must have the wrong room." He backed away.

The lady relaxed and smiled. She leaned on the door frame and delicately pinched the cigarette between extended fingers. "Who you looking for?"

"Did an old man come in here?" he asked boldly.

"Marty!" she called over her shoulder.

Rory's stomach turned. *I blew it now. The old man will come to the door and yell at me.* He was about to bolt.

"Who is it?" asked a voice. A man in green pants and undershirt came up beside the woman. He was mostly bald, but definitely not Seadog.

"You know this kid?"

He shook his head. "You lost, sonny?"

"No." Rory backed right into the far wall. "Sorry to bother you."

"No problem," the lady replied and closed the door.

He slid down to the floor with a groan and sat staring at a bug hanging under the rail across from him. He watched it for a couple of minutes, trying to decide what to do next. *What would James Bond do? He'd have special devices to take readings. A fingerprint kit and a tricorder, at least. Even better would be a light saber! Then I could cut my way right through the wall.*

That's strange, he suddenly thought. *That bug isn't moving. It must be dead. Besides, this place is so clean, I'm amazed they'd have a bug.* He scrambled across the hall and picked at it. It wasn't a bug at all. It was a tiny latch that looked like a pull tab on a soda can. "I never thought to look under the railing," he whispered disgustedly and gave it a pull.

Click!

He jumped back. The wall swung in and opened onto a narrow passage, with a painted metal floor leading to a stairway that went up and down. He swallowed hard, as though he had a bone stuck in his throat.

The passage was brightly lit and so narrow it would probably touch his shoulders on either side. *Do I dare? It isn't actually marked PRIVATE.* He glanced swiftly up and down the hall. The coast was clear. "This is a test of your courage, young Skywalker. Use the force!" Sucking a huge breath of air in through his nose, he took a step into the unknown.

The door swung shut behind him with another click and he let the air out. *This is it!* He crept along the hall to the stairs. *These tunnels probably lead around the entire ship.* With hot cheeks and thumping heart, he headed down. Somehow, he knew it was the right direction. After all, Seadog had been going that way since Rory had started to tail him.

Three flights down the stairs ended, with no door at the end of the hall. Everything was bare sheet metal, with no railing and no carpeting. Rory flattened himself against the stair rail when he spotted Seadog way up ahead, poking in some fuse boxes.

"Target reacquired," he whispered into an imaginary mike on his sleeve and waited until the old man limped out of sight. There was no one else around. "Target moving slowly. I'm on it," he added to his sleeve and started after him. He was so involved in his game that he forgot his fear.

He crept along, the engines thrumming in his ears and vibrating the floor. This was where he had wanted to explore all along. Here were the narrow halls, stuffy hot air, oval hatchways, and painted pipes and control boxes. Passing open doorways on either side of him, he glanced into rooms full of machinery where men were working. Down here they weren't dressed in white uniforms. They had on jeans or overalls.

At one point, Rory had to hide between two storage bins while three crewmen went by. He nearly puked when he heard them coming up behind him. He barely had time to squeeze out of sight. He held his breath until he was sure they were well past him. After that, he kept an eye on his back. . . .

Before he could think twice, Rory was yanked roughly through a hatchway by unseen hands. It happened so fast, he couldn't even squawk. Clammy fingers clapped over his mouth and strong arms held him. The door slammed and with it went most of the light. He was trapped! His heart raced wildly.

"Why are you dogging me, boy?" a raspy voice whispered. *Seadog!*

Rory was petrified. His heart thumped so hard in his ears, he couldn't hear anything else. He struggled hard, but the old man had a strong grip.

"Out with it!" The voice had a terrifying edge. "Are you the demon finally come to claim me?" he hissed. "I'm not afraid."

This guy is a loony. He's going to kill me and no one will hear my screams. The realization gave Rory strength. He kicked and thrashed with all his might, until the old man grunted and let go. Rory leapt out of his reach, panting and gulping. "What do you want?" He tried to sound tough, but his words were squeaky. All he could see were the rims of the old man's glasses and a glint off his teeth and beaky nose.

"Aye, I see the lay of this." The old man's voice was irritated. "You're the clumsy hand who bowled me off my pins at boarding yesterday."

Rory could only nod. He tried desperately to think. His eyes darted to the door behind the crazy old coot.

"What name do you go by?"

"Rory Dugan, sir," he stammered and retreated a couple of unsteady steps until his back met something solid.

"Well, you behave like a common sneak, Mr. Dugan. What do you want of me?"

"Nothing. I was only playing. That's all." He wondered if the old man was going to pull a weapon. As his eyes adjusted to the dimness, he could see him painfully rubbing his ribs through his tweed vest where Rory had jabbed him as he thrashed. He looked like a cigar-chomping gargoyle, with a white ring around his neck. He pinched the cigar out from between his teeth and scratched his chin while he looked Rory over.

"Playing, you say? At what?"

Rory shrugged. "Nothing."

Suddenly, everything changed. Rory was caught once more in the mysterious old man's frightening stare. His black eyes seemed to suck away any light, and left Rory staring down a dark well so deep he was too scared to move. He simply couldn't tear his eyes away for fear of falling. He was peering into the face of a nameless dark terror. A cold so biting that it burned crept up through his feet and legs and into his chest, freezing him to the spot. He felt his forehead tighten and jaws clench, as if his brain were being squeezed. . . .

The vision of Ian plunging in the pool flashed up again, when Rory reached out to save him but couldn't. All he could do was relive the horrible moment of helplessness that took his brother from him. Such a wrenching pang of loss and frustration and anger, *yes anger,* tore at him. *How dare Ian put me through this for all these years! It's not fair!*

Suddenly a light went on and the spell broke. The bitter memories and bone-chilling fear he had just endured receded with the darkness and were gone. They left him drained. It was all he could do to keep from crumpling onto the floor. He felt prickly with sweat.

The old man had flicked on the light and they both blinked as if they were surprised to find themselves there. They were standing in some kind of machine room, with all sorts of wires and transformer-looking things along the walls. Rory was backed against what looked like a huge steel furnace attached to the floor. He steadied himself against it. The closed hatch was only ten feet away, behind the old man.

"I see you are just an ordinary boy at that," the old man croaked. He didn't look quite so spooky in the light. His flinty black eyes had softened slightly and the corners of his wrinkled mouth had turned up. The expression could almost be called pleasant, if his wrinkled noggin didn't remind Rory of a shrunken voodoo head. "Aye, I suppose I was a bit rough on you. Can't be too careful, though. Can't be too careful," he continued, almost kindly. "Traveling with your family, I'll wager. Yes, I see it now. You have a mother. Attractive woman." Hooking a gnarled thumb at himself he said, "Morgan. That's me," and extended a hand.

Rory didn't take it. "I was just playing. Honest," he repeated, as though he were responding to an angry teacher. *The old guy is crazy. He might do anything.* Eagerly eyeing the hatchway, Rory wondered if he should make a run for it. He wanted to say something. Anything! But he was too scared. The old man's words – I'll dance on your graves – played in his head.

Mr. Morgan dropped his hand. "Just so, just so," he agreed. "But, you've no need to fear me, son. Caught me off guard. Can you blame me?" he smiled. But his jagged teeth flashing like uneven gravestones didn't look friendly. "No hard feelings, I hope. I mean, about my temper."

Rory had to admit, at least to himself, that he shouldn't have been following the guy. But that didn't make him feel any better right then. "Can I go?" he finally found wits enough to ask through a parched throat.

"Aye, of course. Nothing to stop you." Mr. Morgan added, "But now that we're mates and all, you won't sound the alarm on old Morgan. I'll allow I weighed in a bit gruff with you, didn't I?" He stroked his chin with the back of his hand.

Rory nodded.

"What a remarkable boy. I mean, that would never do, now, would it?" Morgan winked. "That is, you seem a regular gobby in that outfit and we bluejackets should stick together. Let's say that, for the present, it's important that I keep below the waterline. What they don't know won't hurt them, if you know what I mean."

Rory didn't. But he didn't say it.

"Smart lad." Then, quick as a blink, the dangerous edge was back in the old man's eye. "Mind you don't skulk around me further, though. Or you'll meet my rough side sure as we're standing here. You want something, you come at me broadside. You understand?"

Rory gulped. "Yes, sir."

With a click and a rumble, the big machine behind Rory started rattling and thundering right in his ear. That was the final straw. Even though his legs were jelly, he yelped and made a mad break for the door.

"Don't fret that," Mr. Morgan chuckled. "That's the fuel pump. Goes on and off all the time."

Rory didn't hear any more. He was out the door and down the hall so fast that he tripped twice before reaching the stairs.

An Ally, a Grandmother,
and a Kick in the Pants

Rory wandered around the private crew halls and mulled over what had happened. He was still shaking. That loud noise was too much. He had to run. His knees were skinned where he had fallen and he'd kept looking over his shoulder, half expecting to see the old man chasing him. As he got further away, fear gave some ground to curiosity. He shuddered, remembering the old man's question about a demon. *And why didn't he want anyone knowing what he was doing? For that matter, what was he doing?* But Rory didn't remember anything about the spell the old man had held him in.

He kept moving, as though staying active would burn off his fear. He didn't pay attention to where he was going. The secret tunnels were all the same, reminding him of an ant farm or rabbit warren. They crossed this way and that, and ran all through the ship behind the walls. After getting completely lost, Rory pushed through a door and found himself blinking in the bright sun of Deck 8. The ocean was calm and a cool breeze touched his face. It felt good. It felt safe.

He had surfaced right next to a photo gallery on the promenade, where the passengers bought pictures of themselves having a good time. The deck was crowded with people in bright clothes and sunglasses, lounging in chairs and walking along the wide wooden surface that stretched the length of the ship. All along, opposite the outside railing, were stores, galleries, and arcades. He started to laugh when a really fat old lady, even bigger than Eddie, lowered herself into a deck chair that creaked and complained under her.

Eddie! Oh, no, I forgot to check in! He charged down the three flights of stairs to Deck 11, raced along the hall to his cabin, and casually strolled in as though he were on time.

"Hello?" he called, gulping air to catch his breath.

No answer. *No one here. Whew.* He scribbled a note and left.

Back aloft, he rambled down the promenade again, looking at storefronts distractedly and thinking over his weird encounter with Mr. Morgan. It was almost an hour later and the whole thing didn't seem so frightening. *Still strange, though.* The smell of french fries outside a fish-and-chips stand reached his nose. *Time for lunch.*

"Whatcha doing?" said a voice behind him.

"WHAT?" For the second time that morning, Rory nearly jumped out of his skin. He whipped around. A tall black-haired girl about his own age was standing inches away from him. She had bright red shorts on, a white shirt tied around her skinny waist, and a playful smile. With a pixie haircut, teasing emerald eyes, and her fists on her hips, she looked like an elf from Middle Earth.

"Aren't you the Nervous Neddy." She popped gum.

He shrugged. "I . . . no. You scared me. That's all."

"I can see that. Sticka gum?" She tossed him the pack while she blew a bubble.

Rory took a piece and handed the rest back. "Thanks."

"What's your name?"

"Rory."

"Rory, huh? I'm Lucy Pritchard. I like your sailor suit."

He blushed self-consciously and pushed his glasses up. He wasn't good at talking to girls. This one was kind of pretty. She had a tomboy look about her, too. Being taller than him made it tough looking her straight in the eye. She just stared back.

"Nice eyes, too," she remarked. "Real blue." The corners of her mouth shot up in a pointy grin.

Now she really had him flustered. "What do you want?"

"There's no one to hang out with on this tub and I'm bored stiff," she complained. "There are only about fifteen kids. I scoped them out already. A couple of real sissy girls, a bunch of rugrats, and some bratty little boys. That leaves you and me."

Rory wondered what it left them for. "I'm kinda busy right now."

"I can tell. You been running all over this poop deck."

"Promenade," he corrected automatically. "Don't you know anything about ships?"

She planted her hands back on her hips and chewed slowly. "Well, *excuse* me. It floats, we're stuck here for a week, and the pool is on the top deck. Anything else isn't worth knowing."

Rory disagreed. "Actually, there are some interesting things –"

"Name one," she challenged, full of green-eyed mischief. He hesitated.

"I thought so." She snapped her gum. "I just turned thirteen. How about you?"

"Twelve." He was still trying to think of a comeback. He didn't like being put on the spot by some pushy girl.

"You meet the junior cruise director yet?" She sounded disgusted.

"Last night. She seemed nice."

"Oh, like, gag me. She wants everyone to be friends, so she started some really lame games this morning. I bailed. I didn't see you there?"

Rory had a flash of guilt as he recalled carefully avoiding them all morning. "I didn't go. I was exploring the ship."

"Good move. It had to be better."

"I thought you didn't like ships."

"I don't. I'd rather take a plane. Eating and dying of old age are the hot sports around here. I haven't seen anyone under a hundred, have you? Unless you count the junior cruise queen and a couple of hotties in the crew."

"What about the fireworks last night?"

"Yeah, that was okay. There was a fun disco, too. But that's for night stuff." Lucy paused to pop another huge bubble. "You smell fries?"

"Yeah."

"Wanna get some?"

"Sure. Oh, I don't have any money."

"No sweat. My grams gave me a couple of bucks."

Sitting cross-legged on deck with a basket of fries, Rory decided Lucy Pritchard was okay, but figured she must be really bored if she found him interesting. He was sure that if she were at his school, she'd call him a geek like everyone else. In between ketchupy mouthfuls, Lucy did most of the talking and still managed to get him to open up. Somehow she made him feel like he'd known her a long time.

"So you live in Wichita, huh?" she asked.

"Yup."

"See any tornadoes?"

"A couple."

"That's way cool. I'm from a boring old suburb in Boston. My friend Chloe and me are going to New York and be singers someday."

"I want to be a sailor," he told her.

"No kidding? The Marines, or something?"

"Merchant Marines, maybe, or sailboat skipper."

Lucy stopped chewing. "I bet you're smart, huh?" She waved a hand. "Don't sweat it. I like math and stuff. I just don't spread that around 'cause it's like death, you know? You got a girlfriend?"

He felt his face turn hot and looked down. "I don't even know any girls," he mumbled.

"I bet they know you," she laughed. "There's this guy, Dave, that I like. I think he likes me, too. Chloe's gonna get one of his friends to ask him."

Rory thought he should nod. So he did.

"So where'd you go exploring this morning?"

Without really knowing why, he told her about Mr. Morgan. By the time he got to his close call in the fuel-pump room, he could feel the fear reaching up from inside him again. His voice even cracked a little.

Lucy was impressed. "He actually grabbed you?"

"Yup."

"I would have kicked his butt!"

Rory didn't believe that. "He was pretty scary, you know. He even talks with funny words. Like a sailor from long-ago times." He told her about the dance-on-your-graves remark. "What do you think that means?"

"Beats me. Maybe it's a threat. Or a curse! He didn't say it to *you*, did he?"

Rory shook his head.

"That's lucky." She spit three times on her fingers. "You'd probably be under his spell or something, if he did," she warned, in a hushed voice. "You're cool. I could tell something was up with you when I first spotted you."

Rory's skin tingled, his eyes lit up, and he grinned from ear to ear. No one had ever called him anything but boring, or worse.

"So, what do we do about the old geezer?" she asked.

"I don't know. He said something about a demon being after him."

"He is crazy. You gonna meet him again?"

"Dunno."

She finished her fries and put the gum wad she'd stuck to the paper tray back in her mouth. "Let's go."

"Where to?"

"We'll tail him. If he pulls anything weird, we'll tell the captain."

"Huh?" Rory didn't like the sound of that. Morgan had warned him not to sneak around anymore – and he was scary. "You're kidding, right?"

"Where should we look first?" She wasn't kidding.

"No way. He's dangerous," Rory argued.

Lucy jumped to her feet. "To the scene of the crime!" she cried.

His stomach jumped with her, but the rest of him stayed put. "But . . . we'll get in trouble," he protested. "I barely got away."

"No, we won't. There are two of us now and you know the way," she laughed.

What's next? he thought. *First that old geezer and now this girl.* But he didn't want to admit that he was scared to go back to the pump room.

"What deck was he on?"

"Someone might see us," he warned, as the elevator doors closed them in.

"You kidding? We're a couple of pathetic kids. They'll give us a guided tour and serve ice cream on top!" she replied.

Rory hit the button for Deck 11. "That's the lowest passenger deck. We'll have to take stairs after that. There are four more decks below. All restricted. I know my way around pretty well now," he explained importantly.

When they got off, he didn't show her the secret doorways. They were still his secret. They stopped at one of those forbidding-looking doors marked PERSONNEL ONLY. "See?

This door leads to a crew stairway. But we can't go in there." He really wanted her to turn back.

Lucy flashed a grin, popped her gum, and barged in. She didn't even check to see if anyone was around.

Rory's heart sank. A new terror had taken over his life. Its name was Lucy Pritchard. *Why did I have to tell her about Mr. Morgan?* he asked himself. *Don't I already have enough trouble?* He looked over his shoulder and crept down the steps after her. *As long as we keep quiet. . . .*

"What deck do we want?" she yelled up to him, her voice echoing in the stairwell. Rory winced.

"This one." He pointed to the door at Deck 14. "There is a lot of sensitive machinery here and we should be careful not to –"

Lucy shoved through and signaled for him to follow. He shook his head.

"Come on, or we'll get caught."

His feet were bolted to the spot. *This is where I draw the line!*

"Which way?"

Rory still didn't budge.

"Are you chicken?" She flapped her arms.

Yes, he was. But he was more chicken to let on that he was. He stepped out into a loud and crammed hallway, much like the one that Morgan had yanked him off of. *This is a big mistake.* Yet, there he was, loping along after her.

"Hold on, you two," a deep voice boomed right behind them.

They stopped. With mush for legs and his heart thumping like crazy, Rory knew he couldn't make a break for it. They both turned slowly around.

Standing over them was a burly officer in a white uniform, peaked cap, and a jelly donut in his hand. His thin mouth was a stern line under a caterpillar mustache. For some reason he reminded Rory of his gym teacher, when he was about to torture the class by making them climb ropes or wrestle.

Lucy smiled, as though he'd given them money. "Hi. We just wanted to see the engine room. Is that okay?"

Is that okay? That's like asking if it's okay to write in a library book, or okay to skip school. We're cooked – as good as deep-fried.

But the most amazing thing happened. The man smiled. It wasn't much of a smile, but Rory wasn't picky.

"I'm Officer Bergeron." He had a French accent. "The signs upstairs say PERSONNEL ONLY. I am not remembering either of you at crew briefings."

Rory was about to confess when Lucy broke in. "We'll sign on if you show us around."

Bergeron took a bite of his donut and studied his two prisoners. Rory tried not to look too guilty. "What are your names?" he asked.

"I'm Lucy and this is Rory." She aimed a thumb his way.

"There is custom, *n'est-ce pas?* You cannot sneak in here uninvited. You must first to see the purser and he will arrange tours." He waved his hand towards the door and the two kids headed back to the stairs. Rory was relieved that there was no mention of telling his mother.

"Where's the purser?" Lucy asked.

"Deck 10, off the main lobby."

"Can't you make an exception?" she pleaded, with her brightest smile. "We won't tell anyone that you bent a rule."

Bergeron shook his head. He escorted them to the stairs and told them not to go below Deck 11.

"I guess that means there's no ice cream, huh?" Rory whispered sarcastically.

"Is that all boys think about?" she whispered back.

"It's better than getting into trouble with the law."

She gave his shoulder a shove. "Come on."

He followed her up nine decks. *This is exhausting.* She wound around the halls to her stateroom. It was a nicer deck than his – wider halls, paintings on the walls, no overhead pipes, and well above sea level.

Lucy slid her key through the slot and pushed in. Rory waited in the hall.

"Hi, Grams!" Lucy called. "Anyone home?"

"You needn't yell, Lucille." A woman's voice came from far inside the room. "This tiny room would fill up from a whisper."

"Can we have ice creams?" Rory heard her ask.

"We? Have you sprouted a second head?" asked the voice.

"Huh? Rory, get in here."

Rory stepped into the room. It was larger than his cabin and had a small deck outside a sliding glass door, which made it sunny and seem even bigger. Rory decided Lucy must be rich. Like his cabin, it was cluttered with clothes and things strewn everywhere, but it smelled of girls' stuff like skin cream and perfume.

Sitting on a deck chair outside was a round-faced old lady. Skinny like Lucy, she was wearing jeans, a flowery blouse, and a straw hat over curly white hair. "You go by Rory?"

"Yes. Rory Dugan." He cast a sidelong glance at Lucy, who was rooting through the fridge.

"I'm Mrs. Donnelly. Pleased to meet you. A good Irish lad like you is certainly welcome in my home, such as it is." She beckoned him onto the balcony with both hands, then took off her sunglasses to take a good look at him. Her delighted green-eyed gaze put him at ease in the way Lucy's chatter had. "Are you coming from Ireland, too?"

Rory leaned way over the balcony to look at the ocean far below. He wished his cabin were up this high. "We were in England for a vacation."

"Did you like it?"

"It was very elucidating," Rory told her.

"Indeed." Grams looked confused and Rory wondered if he'd picked the right word.

"Grams took me to Ireland to visit where she lived when she was a girl," explained Lucy. She was chomping on something crunchy. "What about ice cream, Grams?"

"Do I look like the Good Humor man?" Grams hadn't taken her smiling eyes off Rory. "So, tell me, Rory, which county were your people from?"

"I don't know. I was born in Detroit and named after my great-grandpa."

"Well, I left Dublin as a young girl, not much older than Lucy, and I haven't been back in fifty years. I wanted the child to see it before I die. Unfortunately, her mother couldn't get the time off work to join us."

"Grams won't fly. That's why we're on this stupid barge," Lucy added.

Grams ignored her. "Are you traveling with your parents?"

"My mom and stepdad, ma'am."

"Take note, Lucille. The young man has what are called manners. They might come in handy if you learned about them someday."

Lucy rolled her eyes. "I know what manners are. Tell her Rory."

Rory blushed. "I ... what?" He had no idea what she was talking about.

"The officer guy! I was real polite, wasn't I?"

"Pestering the crew, then, were you?" Grams teased.

"Rory's the one who slammed into some guy like a hockey player! Tell her Rory."

It crossed his mind to run and never look back. He nervously pushed his glasses up.

"Don't let her ride you like that," Grams laughed. "She has a streak in her that will be her undoing one day. Tell the poor lad you're teasing before he bursts."

Lucy laughed.

Rory mumbled something about knowing that all along. But it made him feel stupid and off balance. He could see that Lucy liked to make trouble.

"Anyway, it's up deck, or topside, or whatever you call it, for me," Grams said, getting up. "I'll leave you to look after my Lucy. See that she doesn't get too wild." She grabbed a big straw handbag from the bed and headed for the door. "I'll let you both in on a secret as long as you don't tell where you heard it," she whispered loudly. "Somewhere on this barge, as you call it, Lucy, there is enough ice cream to make you sick. And it's all free for kids. You've only to ask."

The two looked at each other and grinned.

Sunning by the top deck pool, with ice cream dripping from a cone onto his hand, was one of life's perfect moments for Rory. Lucy talked endlessly about her friends, school, and whatever came into her mouth. Rory was happy to listen. He preferred it. As she babbled on, he pictured her busy home life with her brothers and friends and wondered what it would be like to be surrounded by all that activity. His house was kind of quiet.

"So what's your room at home like?" she asked. "Bet you've got pictures of spaceships and glow-in-the-dark stars on the ceiling, right?"

That was a surprise. "What's wrong with that?" he asked. "Anyway, they're regular ships. I've got a neat tele-scope that I can see the neighborhood with, too. My mom thinks I'm looking at Jupiter."

"*Oooh*, Rory. You looking in girls' windows?" she giggled.

He turned purple. "Am not. I meant backyards and the park down the street."

"You're a Peeping Tom!" she teased.

"Am not."

"Guess what my room looks like."

Rory thought about it for a second, glad she'd changed the subject. "It's all pink and covered in pop star posters. You've got one of those fur-covered antique-style phones and heart-shaped photos glued to your mirror."

She made barfing noises. "As if! What movie did you rip that from?"

They were finishing their third cone each. They had both missed lunch, except for the french fries, of course.

"I'm going to try pistachio licorice almond fudge next," Rory declared.

"I'll have pepperoni and sausage with mint chips."

Rory belched.

"There's manners for you," Lucy scolded, and added such a long deep growling burp of her own that he sat up and stared at her. He'd never heard a girl do that. The grossest thing he'd ever seen was Tommy Smart turning his eyelids inside out.

"That's what my dad would call a real dribbler," he laughed. He took another lick of his ice cream and suddenly felt sick. *Maybe I won't have a fourth cone. Of any flavor. Maybe I'll never eat again.* Then he remembered his mom. "Uh-oh. I gotta go."

"What for?"

"I forgot to check back with my mom." He got up, ice cream smeared on his hands, face, and shirt.

"Will your mom mind you wearing so much ice cream?"

He looked at his hands and groaned. "Now I'm going to get the lecture on saving room for supper on top of the one for being irresponsible and forgetful." He knew them all by heart. "What should I do?"

"Here," Lucy said, pointing to the pool. "You can wash off. Then they'll never know. Just pick at your food like you're seasick, or something. They'll give you sympathy instead of a lecture. I do it all the time."

"You mean, lie to my mom?"

Lucy burst into laughter. "What planet are you from? Don't you ever tell your mom fibs?"

Rory blushed. "Not really."

"Now is a good time to start. Come on, lean over the pool and wash off."

This wouldn't be easy. He'd managed to avoid swimming by telling Lucy he just wanted ice cream. But she'd know something was up if he looked too scared to wash off in the pool.

With shaky hands, Rory got down on his knees, carefully laid his glasses beside him, and leaned way over the edge to put his face close to the water. *So far, so good.* He felt a little woozy, but he wasn't going to let on that he was scared to death.

Lucy stood behind him. Suddenly, he felt her foot against his butt and a hard push.

"Hey!" *Splash!*

His face hit the water first and he went down like a rock. In an instant he was up again, spluttering and scrambling for the side of the pool in a real panic. He climbed out, water streaming from his clothes, his heart racing, and feeling like a soaked dog. Lucy was laughing so hard she was doubled over. He wiped water off his face and shoved his glasses back on his nose. He tried as hard as he could to hide his fear. He didn't want her to know that falling in the water was worse to him than falling in a snake pit. But it was reflected in Lucy's guilty expression. The smile fell off her face.

"Are you alright?" she stammered. "Did you hit your head? I'm sorry. It's only water."

Only water, yeah, right. Rory bit back on his temper. He saw nothing in her eyes but humor and so he laughed a bit, too.

She smiled, glad he wasn't mad. "At least you're clean enough for dinner now," she giggled nervously. "Uh-oh. Don't look now. Cruise queen alert!"

Rory glanced over his shoulder and saw the junior cruise director across the pool.

"Let's drift!" said Lucy. They grabbed their stuff and split, Rory squelching along in his wet sneakers and feeling surprised at how little he cared about what just happened.

An Old Photo

Rory did what Lucy had suggested. He lied. He told his mom that he felt seasick, and picked through dinner as though it were raw eggs. It worked like a charm. Mom didn't scold him for not showing up all day. Then she sent him to their cabin to lie down, while she and Eddie went to some boring play in one of the ship's theaters. As soon as the coast was clear, he lit out to the promenade and watched a Mardi Gras, which was a huge parade with costumes, fireworks, and music. Then he played a couple of video games at the arcade and got back to the cabin in time to have it all to himself for a while.

In his pajamas, he flopped on his bed and booted up his laptop computer. His dad had given him the computer a year ago and everything in his world was on it: his secret journal, video games, web pages, homework, and, best of all, everything he had collected about the *Titanic*. He couldn't even explain why he loved the *Titanic*. She fascinated a lot of people more than any other ship – maybe because she was thought to be unsinkable, or that she was so magnificent. Rory, with his fear of water, couldn't help considering how the line between life and death was drawn so cleanly by the ocean's surface.

He listened to the hard drive *whirr* and *click*, while thinking about the incredible day he'd had. *New friends, mysteries, and adventures.* It was better than anything he could have made up. He wondered if the first day aboard the *Titanic* was as exciting.

I'm going to E-mail Dad about it, he decided. Rory wished he lived with his dad because Dad's girlfriend, Tanya, was fun and they had a pool table and big TV and didn't mind if he messed the place up, or talked about ships and computers. He wanted to learn all about his father's software business so he could work there, and to go sailing together like they had one time before. It was one of the best memories he had. *I'm going to sail around the world on my own boat someday,* he promised himself. *Then no one can find me.*

The cursor blinked, waiting for his command. He loved this. The computer was his comfort zone, a place where he was in control. He understood its world and he was sure it understood him, too. The rules were simple and the computer never let him down. That gave him confidence. He could go on-line and talk in chat groups or LISTSERVS, and nobody knew or cared he was only twelve. No one put him down or told him he didn't belong, so he wasn't self-conscious. The group members accepted him for himself, as a ship enthusiast, not how they thought he should be because of his age or looks. That was what was strange about Lucy. She seemed to accept him without judging his geeky haircut and shy manner. She was hard to figure out.

He clicked automatically to the *Titanic* "scrapbook" his father had scanned in for him. It had every news clipping, picture, blueprint, and reference to the *Titanic* that they could find. That included a bunch of web sites that they had completely reconstructed on his hard drive.

Rory's favorite challenge was naming all the pictures on a *Titanic* flash card program. He loaded up and clicked START. The scene changed randomly every three seconds. He tested himself by seeing how quickly he could identify the caption, or name the people, in each photo.

The first picture came up: a man in uniform with a white mustache and whiskers. *Easy!* "Captain Edward John Smith," he rapped out.

Next, an ocean liner in dock. "SS *Carpathia*, rescuer of the survivors."

Several boys on a deck near a hopscotch board. "The children's play area."

A huge room filled with white linen and crystal-covered tables and a staircase at the far end. "Main dining room," he said, and thought the dining room of the *Sea Lion* was plain compared to it.

A newspaper photo of two couples flashed up next. "Survivors, Mr. & Mrs. Edward Lowrey. Unidentified couple in background."

Next picture: liner at sea. "Rear view of *Titanic* departing from Southampton." He remembered yesterday afternoon's departure.

That's strange, he thought, *something seems different.*

Next picture. "Lifeboat #13 alongside *Carpathia*," he said automatically. *What could be different?*

Next. "Molly Brown, a journalist who survived." *It was in that picture of the Lowreys. . . .*

Next. A fancy room with stuffed chairs and pillars in the middle. "Reading room," he said, not paying attention anymore. It switched again.

Rory stopped the program. Keying back five pictures, he came to the shot of Mr. and Mrs. Edward Lowrey. There were four people in the picture. The Lowreys stood in front and another couple behind. He'd seen this picture many times. But this time, he thought he recognized the man in the back. *That's what's different.* Hair prickled the back of his neck as he magnified the image.

"No way!"

The picture was grainy and he couldn't be sure. But it looked like him.

"No way," he whispered again. He rubbed his eyes and took a fresh look. The picture was still there. *This is impossible! Like something out of The X-Files.* He scratched his head.

Rory's stomach growled. He was regretting that he had pretended to be sick at supper. He rummaged through the little fridge and found a bagel. Taking it back to his computer, he took another look at the picture.

"I've got to talk to Lucy. This is impossible." He began pacing, wondering if he should go find her. He didn't dare chance it. *Mom and Eddie might be home any minute.* He turned to stare at the picture on the screen.

There, staring back, complete with a cigar stub lodged between his teeth, was Mr. Morgan. Standing behind Mrs. Lowrey, in his funny suit, his angry eyes blazing at the camera, he looked exactly as he had that morning!

Rory felt a chill brush by his face, like a freezer opening and closing. A fear settled briefly on his shoulders and he sat down, almost dizzy. He knew there was danger here. He just didn't know what. . . .

5

A Precarious Friendship

Rory had a terrible night. He tossed fitfully, dreaming over and over about jumping into the pool to save Ian. When he pulled him to safety, Ian turned into the old man. Before he could dive back in, Ian had sunk out of sight, beneath the surface. And every time he did this, the old man would laugh and say, "Save yourself. Save yourself."

He woke up dripping with sweat and panting. He squinted at his watch. It was just after seven. *What a nightmare! It felt like I didn't sleep at all.* As he shook it off and tried to think about where he really was, his discovery of the night before tumbled back into his thoughts. *Why was Morgan in my dream?*

Before he did anything else, Rory crammed his glasses on his face and booted up the computer to take another look at that picture. While it loaded, he looked at the map of the Atlantic Ocean he had taped over his sofa bed to chart the *Sea Lion's* progress. *We're about 500 miles west of*

France, he calculated, and drew a mark. That was a long ways out in the ocean. With all that had happened so far, Rory couldn't believe he'd been aboard only one full day.

After a few mouse clicks, up popped the picture of the Lowreys and there was Morgan, still staring back with his flinty glare and tiny glasses. His age and appearance were so much like yesterday morning that Rory got the shivers.

I've got to tell Lucy right away! He dressed in jeans and T-shirt, figuring he'd slip out for a while before his parents got up. Even though they hadn't made a big deal about it, he knew they were burned up over his not checking in all day yesterday. As he reached for the door handle, it clicked and popped open on its own.

"Mom!" He stepped back in surprise.

"Good morning," she replied and tripped in balancing a tray of Danish pastries and coffee. Dressed in calf-length black slacks and white blouse, Rory was always amazed at how she took such care to look great, and at the same time was such a slob. She spilled everything. "And where are you off to, young man?" she asked.

"Can I go see Lucy for a while?"

"What do you need to see her for right now?" She looked around for a place to put the tray.

Rory waited, wondering what she would do. The cabin was so messy, there was nowhere to put it down. Every available space was covered with clothing and junk. With a quick movement of her elbow, she cleared off one end of the dresser. Makeup, clothes, trash, and games all clattered to the floor. Rory smiled. *That's my mom.*

"I've got to tell her something," he continued, with a giggle.

She didn't seem to notice his amusement. "It can wait. I want to spend the morning as a family." She passed him a cup and a pastry and sat down next to him on his bed.

He groaned. It was on the tip of his tongue to argue, but he didn't. He wasn't sure how to explain what had happened. "Is this breakfast?" His rumbling gut was reminding him of how little he had eaten in the past day.

"No. We'll go up to the buffet when Eddie gets back. I bet you're starved."

"I am," he agreed. "Where'd he go?"

"To get some fresh air. He isn't sleeping too well. Being on the ship is making him a bit sicker than he thought it would. This is his first sea voyage, too, you know."

"Why did he pick a boat then?"

"Because it's romantic."

"With me along?"

His mom gave him one of those looks that said he was asking a stupid question. "As soon as he gets back, we'll go to breakfast. Sound good?"

Rory nodded. He dunked the pastry in his coffee and took a big bite. He felt his chest tighten. "Mom, can I show you something?"

"Shoot."

He flipped the lid of his laptop open and showed her the picture. "You see that guy in the back?"

She nodded.

"That's the old guy I knocked down in the lobby when we boarded."

She looked closer. "So it is. Where is this picture from?"

He took a deep breath. "These are *Titanic* survivors on the dock in New York in 1912."

Claire looked doubtful. She grinned and her eyebrows rose a mile in the air, as though waiting for a punch line to a joke. It didn't come. "Oh, Rory, you and your imagination."

He expected that and showed her the backup information that went along with the picture to prove that it was a news clipping from 1912. Once she was convinced, she looked at Morgan again.

"It does look like him, but obviously it can't be," she said, with calm assurance. "A relative, maybe."

He was surprised at how relieved he was to hear her say that. "Yeah," he agreed. "That must be it." He cringed as she dropped her Danish in the coffee and sloshed it all over her pants. *That's my mom.*

After she changed, Eddie came back and they all headed upstairs to the grand dining room, right in the heart of the ship. It was practically deserted. At night, when it was crowded and noisy and all lit up with crystal globes and table lamps, it felt a lot smaller. Now it was an echo chamber and everyone spoke quietly, as though they were in church. The breakfast buffet spread out in the center seemed miles away from their table, and the few other passengers that were up that early looked like dots in an ocean.

Rory's stomach rumbled again as soon as he smelled the waffles, pancakes, eggs, and meats. All three of them piled their plates full and carted them back to their table.

Topping up on seconds of sausages and syrup, Rory wondered how best to ask his mom again if he could hang out with Lucy that morning. But, before he could plan a strategy, Eddie started in.

"I guess you should stick close to us this A.M., sport," he announced between forkfuls of omelette. "I mean, we trusted you to check in yesterday and what happened? Besides, your mom would like to spend some time as a family."

Rory glowered. He had hoped that Poundcake wouldn't give him a hard time. *Fat chance. Very fat.* "You weren't there, so I left a note around lunchtime."

"You should have come to find us," Eddie insisted. "We needed your mom's key card back."

"How was I supposed to know you got locked out?" Rory poured a pleading look all over his mom. It worked.

"Now, Eddie, let's just get through breakfast," she said.

"He has to learn some responsibility. After all, I'm the father here and –"

"No, you're not," Rory interrupted. "This is the first fun I've had on this boring trip. I didn't want to go to England. You just don't like –"

Claire cut in. "We are sharing a very small cabin. Can't you two get along even once?" She rubbed her head.

An unpleasant silence hung in the air while Eddie and Rory stewed.

Rory was about to try again when the junior cruise director appeared at their table. She was a blonde college-age woman, all smiles and dressed like a gym teacher, complete with whistle around her neck. "Hi!" she beamed excitedly, as though what she said was the most inviting thing ever uttered. "I'm Judy. We didn't see you folks much yesterday. You're Rory, aren't you?" She practically pinched his cheek. He practically tossed up his first helpings.

"We're the Farentinos," Claire said. "Can I help you?"

"Well!" Judy said breathlessly. "My job is to make sure all the kids have a great time and we've got some swell activities lined up for today. Will you be joining us, Rory?" She looked at Claire when she said this.

"*Um,* this morning we're going to do things as a family," Rory explained, never so thankful for an excuse before in all his life. "But maybe I can hook up with you later?"

Judy took a deep breath like she was going to blow up a balloon. "I sure hope you will! The other kids are having such a great time, we wouldn't want you to miss out," she said, all in the same breath.

"Okay," Rory agreed.

She tousled his hair and told him they would be "mustering on the pool deck at 0100 sharp."

After she left, Eddie affectionately cuffed Rory's shoulder. "We're going to do things as a family. . . . Bet you never ate crow that fast in your life before."

Rory's shoulders started to shake and the three of them broke out laughing.

For the next couple of hours, he shadowed them around the ship. Besides the promenade and some art galleries, there was a shopping mall inside – it was set up like an old-fashioned street, with cobblestones and gas lamps and street musicians and jugglers. Then there was an amusement park with some small rides and a fun house. They avoided the prearranged games and activities like dance class and sing-alongs. His parents were as bored by that idea as he was, although the activities looked well attended.

Along the way, Rory spotted Mr. Morgan on Deck 10, still dressed in that old suit. *Maybe it's the only one he has.* "There he is over there," he whispered to his mother. He thought about his dream and was dying to know what the old man was doing.

"It's not polite to point at people" was all she said, but he noticed her giving him a good once-over. Rory could have sworn he heard the old man whistling a tune.

After that, Rory begged to be let off the leash. "Mom, can I please go?" he whined. "This is so boring. And I've got stuff to do."

"What stuff?"

"Stuff! You know. Stuff." He shuffled around and made faces.

"That's right, there's a yodeling competition up on the lido deck in a half hour." Eddie laughed. Rory stuck out his tongue. Eddie did it back.

"Alright, alright," Claire sighed, practically laughing. "But meet us for lunch."

"I promise."

"At the ship museum," Eddie insisted.

"Okay." Rory charged off down the deck before they could change their minds. He raced straight to Lucy's cabin. No one was there. *Rats!* He tried the pool deck and anywhere else she might be. No luck.

Without really realizing it, Rory found himself being drawn aft of Deck 10. Morgan was still there. He was across from some cabins, at a mooring station, taking stock of several big white bins along the wall. There was an open area with open windows looking over the back of the ship. *Kind of where the poop deck would be on a wooden frigate,* Rory thought. Looking over the edge, he saw the water behind the ship being churned up by the engines and leaving a huge wake.

He felt a knot twist in his stomach as soon as he saw the old man. Wary of Morgan's temper, part of him wanted to leave. He was both frightened and insatiably curious, especially now that he had seen him in that photo. Rory stood guardedly near a huge capstan, with chain as thick as his arm wrapped round it that attached to an anchor hanging over the side.

After a bit, Morgan looked up and squinted at him. "Come on out, Mr. Dugan," he croaked. "Needn't hang back. We're mates."

Rory stepped out cautiously. "What are you doing?" he asked, trying to sound casual.

"What's it look like?"

"Checking the respirators?" Rory guessed.

"Smart lad."

"Do you work on the ship?"

"At my age?"

"Then, how come you're doing this?"

"Need to be primed if there's a fire," Morgan explained matter-of-factly.

"Are you worried about a fire?" Rory was suddenly worried about fire.

Morgan paused and looked like he was considering the question. He smiled. "Where's that pretty girl you were courting yesterday? I'll wager she's better fare than a nasty old sailor like me."

Rory blushed. "I couldn't find her."

The old man seemed to be in a much better mood than Rory had ever seen him. Both his tone and manner were gentler. He chuckled. "Aye. I see the lay of this. You're a lone seabird like me." He tossed a gas mask back into a bin and marked something off in his book. "Don't set much store in the company of others."

"It's easier to be alone," Rory admitted.

"I know, I know. Don't have to count on anyone else. Master of your own," Morgan agreed. "No one to let down, neither."

That was true. "That's what's so neat about sailing," Rory added. "I'd love to live on the sea."

Morgan sat down on a ladder, letting out a comfortable sigh as though he'd just scratched an itch. He laid his hat beside him, took off his jacket, and started to methodically clean his spectacles. Doing these things made him look much less like a spook than before. Just a very old and brittle man. "Done much sailing, then?"

Rory perched on the capstan beside him. "Once with my dad," he said. "But I live in Kansas. Have you?"

"Spent my life at sea," Morgan said. "Nothing like it. Pitting yourself, man and ship, against the elements. Nothing even compares. But watch out, mind. She's fickle, is the sea. Turn on you in a trice."

Rory couldn't agree more. He often thought that it was a strange thing to want to live on the sea and be afraid of water, all at the same time.

"If you're not frightened of her, you're a fool and make no mistake," Morgan continued, as if reading Rory's thoughts. "Many a sailor is afraid of water. Why, when I was young, most sailors never learned to swim."

Really? I thought it was just me. Rory had tried so hard to forget. But the previous day's dunk was a fresh reminder: it only takes a split second to drown. He looked at Morgan with new eyes, wondering what else the old man might have guessed about him. He felt a connection to this strange old sailor – so different from yesterday in the pump room, or from a ghost on the *Titanic*.

Morgan scratched his whiskers. "It's the same with all us mariners. A true love and hate relationship."

Us mariners, Rory thought proudly. It made him feel like part of a special club for the first time, instead of an outsider. Rory imagined Morgan at sea. *Probably a captain or an admiral, ordering sailors around the deck of a destroyer.*

As they sat there, Morgan told Rory tales of life aboard ship, and how to spot weather changes. Rory was enchanted. He didn't interrupt except to ask the odd question. He didn't want the old man to stop.

Suddenly, Morgan got up, grabbed his jacket and hat, and motioned Rory with a nod to follow him. "Let me show you a few things." He poked along the hall and pushed through a PERSONNEL ONLY door into a tiny gray room with an elevator and narrow stairway. Rory eagerly followed.

"What's your opinion of *Sea Lion*, Mr. Dugan? From one sailor to another," Morgan asked, as he hit the DOWN button with his cane.

Rory wasn't sure he'd heard right. No one had ever wanted his opinion before, except on-line of course. "Well . . . um, liners are a class of their own," he replied nervously and imitated the old man's gesture of rubbing his chin with the back of his hand, as though there were whiskers there. "But, I was thinking yesterday that she's like a freighter with a hotel plopped on top."

"A freighter, you say? I suppose we *are* cargo," Morgan allowed. "Would you say she's safe enough?"

"She meets all the SOLAS regulations," Rory said importantly. He was referring to the international Safety Of Life At Sea standards.

"Can't say I put much faith in them," Morgan replied. "Regs are only minimums. No, I agree with your assessment. Hotel first, seaworthy second."

The elevator door slid open. There was barely enough room for both of them in the tiny metal box. Very different from the wood-paneled passenger cars, with brass railings and mirrored walls. They squeezed in and Morgan pushed the Deck 15 button. That was further down than Rory had been yet. He licked his lips.

Morgan picked his teeth with his tongue. "Air travel has made crossings like this obsolete. That concerns me. Makes shipbuilders sloppy and captains have to avoid hard seas because their ships can't handle them. They wallow around from port to port so the passengers can gamble and drink."

"You think the *Sea Lion* is unsafe?"

"That's what we need to find out."

But before Rory could ask why, the elevator stopped.

"This is the deck where everything important happens," Morgan said, and hobbled out onto a steel deck right across from a couple of closed doors. He tried the handle on one. Rory could hear men's voices, but this time he wasn't worried. He was sure that the old man had a pass to the whole ship. The engines were so loud here that he could feel the churning of the propellers in the water under his feet. It was magical.

"What are we doing here?"

Morgan turned the door handle and smiled. "We are right above the engine pods," he explained, as he pushed the door open.

Rory went in first. It was a tiny control room, covered in gauges and dials and computers, with barely enough room for the two of them. Monitors with blue screens full of numbers and others with closed-circuit video watched different parts of the ship. It was fantastic and he wanted to savor every second.

Morgan sat Rory in the swivel chair in the middle of the room and started explaining the function of many of the controls and how they related to the ship's operation. Rory felt truly privileged. It was like being in command of a nuclear sub, or on the bridge of the *Titanic*. He imagined being Captain Smith and Mr. Morgan as Chief Officer Henry Wilde. *Six points to starboard,* he said to himself and watched the monitor for icebergs. *Radio the bridge for clearance.*

When Morgan finished talking, Rory realized he had hardly heard a word.

"Do you think that instrument failure might have contributed to sinking the *Titanic?*" he asked.

A chill fell on the tiny room and Morgan's face hardened to stone. "What! Instrument failure? On the *Titanic?*" He spat the words out.

Rory instantly regretted the question. The old man's sunken eyes suddenly blazed again. Rory had met this side of him before and wasn't happy to see it. "*Um* . . . I read somewhere about faulty rivets and even a theory about navigation problems?" he said.

"Poppycock!" Morgan's shoulders stiffened. "There were design problems alright. But the simple truth is that her captain didn't respect the sea." He ground the words out between his teeth. "Nothing is unsinkable. Captain Smith and the White Star Line forgot that for a night. The asses imagined they were immune to nature."

Rory didn't understand how the old man could be angry one minute and nice as nachos the next.

"So why is it that she has been sailing in people's memories all these years hence?" Morgan's angry voice crackled with frustration. "Why can't we forget her? Allow her to rest like the thousands of other shipwrecks that rot the sea-lanes from here to the Straits of Magellan? I'll tell you why! Arrogance! Arrogance and pride, that's why. That's what sank her! And it is pride that has kept her so long remembered."

Rory could feel his fear creeping up from his toes, through his veins, and making his scalp tingle. He wanted to melt into the floor. Anything to get away. Suddenly, the door burst open and they both spun their heads in surprise. Filling the doorway was a flabby crewman in greasy overalls and gloves. He looked as stunned by them as they were by him.

"Hey! What are you two doing here?" he demanded. But when he looked at Morgan, his face suddenly changed. The room went ice-cold, like a midwinter window had just been opened. Rory noticed a faint foul odor and wondered if it was an open meat locker that made it so cold. He watched the workman's expression get dark, followed by a look of helplessness and fright. His eyes seemed to shrink into his fat cheeks as though he was in a trance and couldn't tear away. Morgan had the same fixed gaze, only it looked – *what was the word?* – sinister. *Yeah, that's it. Sinister.* Then, as quickly, they both snapped out of it, looking dazed and embarrassed. It all happened so fast, Rory couldn't be sure it was even real.

Morgan spoke first. With a cough, his tone changed from anger to complete confusion. He bent his back and blinked and scratched at his head. He appeared so fragile, it almost seemed that his clothes were holding him up. "I'm sorry," he mumbled in a cracked voice, his hands quivering. "I'm a bit lost and the boy is simple. Could you direct us to the pool? We thought this was the elevator." He smiled like an idiot, pushing his yellow teeth out into a huge overbite. Rory might have laughed if it wasn't so weird.

"You have no business down here, folks," the crewman explained, in a sweat, despite how cold it had turned. "Take the elevator back up, or I'll report you."

"Thank you, young man. Very kind. Are you the lift operator?"

"Are you crazy, old man?" the workman asked. "Did you hear what I said?" There was a touch of fear in his voice.

"My grandson will help you with that. I take two," Morgan replied calmly and patted Rory affectionately on the head. "I really should be more careful with my medications, though," he added absently. "When do you serve dinner?"

The crewman looked disgusted with them both. "Come with me," he ordered. He escorted them to the elevator and sent them up with a warning not to come back below Deck 11 again. Morgan assured him that the service was bad enough to keep him away.

As the elevator rose, Rory kept his head down, wondering what kind of crazy thing Mr. Morgan would do next. He was very confused. He thought about the creepy look on the crewman's face, as though he had seen a ghost. It was oddly familiar, but he didn't know why.

He looked up and saw the old man cackling quietly to himself. "Whenever you find yourself in a tight place, act stupid, feeble, or crazy," he laughed. "Everyone will get out of your way."

A Storm at Sea

ory was more confused than ever. Something really strange was going on inside him. He was having eerie feelings and thoughts that seemed detached and not even his own. And every time he tried to focus on one, it would fade, like a familiar smell that you don't quite recognize or a name you're trying to remember. *As soon as I can, I've got to find Lucy. She'll know what to do.* First thing, though, was to meet Mom and Eddie at the ship museum. When he arrived, they weren't there yet.

The museum was pretty neat. A big pale blue room, with glass cases of scale models of ships through the ages and ancient nautical artifacts. The *Titanic* wasn't there. On the walls hung descriptions and pictures of the inner workings, and he prided himself on already knowing most of the information. There was even a replica of the *Sea Lion*. It was twelve feet long and had every detail crafted into it. Miniature officers stood in the window of the bridge and tiny passengers were placed along the promenade. His eye drifted to the mooring deck he just came from and saw the little anchor hanging over the side of the railing where he'd been sitting with Morgan. Then he counted portholes down to the waterline to figure out where his cabin was.

"See those propellers?" said a familiar chalkboard voice behind him. Eddie waddled up with his mom. She looked like a potato stick next to him. And he looked like the whole potato. Rory turned his eyes back to the four black props underneath the stern of the ship. They were attached to torpedo-shaped pods that hung on poles from the hull. He nodded.

"Well, they shape 'em in those bullet things like that so they flow smooth through the water," Eddie explained. "Inside each tube is a shaft that connects to the engine in the ship."

"No, they don't," Rory disagreed scornfully. "They're called azipods. A whole engine is inside each one and they work like outboard motors."

Eddie's jaw stiffened. "That's stupid. You can't get a whole engine for a ship this size into one of those little things," he said.

"Yes, you can. Anyone knows that," Rory insisted. He had the Poundcake cold on this one. Eddie's bull made him so mad sometimes that he couldn't help himself. He wanted to like him, wanted to get along, if just for his mom. But it was hard.

"Stop it, you two," Claire broke in.

"Well, there's no way to prove it, anyway," Eddie continued smugly.

That did it. Rory pointed to a display on a nearby wall. It was titled THE AZIPOD ENGINE and explained in detail what Rory had said.

"Well, there are others that are how I said," Eddie grumbled, after looking at it. Then they both sulked.

"I'm going to need an aspirin if you two keep this up," said Claire.

"Hi, Rory!" chimed a girl's voice behind him.

They all looked around to see Lucy and Grams standing there in identical white deck pants, sandals, *Show No Fear!* on their T-shirts, and huge sunglasses. It was clear to Rory that they were having much more fun than he was.

"Hi," he replied. He could feel his heartbeat speed up. He hoped that Mom and Eddie didn't embarrass him.

Grams laughed. "Neither love nor money would get Lucille to set foot in here. Then she caught sight of you through the glass."

"Who are your friends, dear?" Claire asked.

Words stuck in Rory's throat. For a second, he couldn't remember his mother's name.

"I'm Claire Farentino, Rory's mother." She extended a hand to Grams. "And this is my husband, Eddie."

"Abigail Donnelly," said Grams and they all shook hands. "This is my granddaughter, Lucy Pritchard. She picked Rory up yesterday and they've been best mates ever since."

"You didn't mention you got engaged yesterday, Rory," Eddie teased.

Rory felt his face turn bright red. He wished Eddie were dead and buried.

"Rory's not my boyfriend." Lucy grinned. Then she raised her eyebrows a couple of times and added, "Yet."

Now he wished she were buried with him.

"What do you make of all these ships, Mr. Farentino?" Grams asked.

"Amazing attention to detail. Especially the engines," Eddie replied dryly.

"Can Rory chow with us this aft?" Lucy asked. "There's a wicked buffet on the pool deck." She smiled slyly at Rory. "Ever been there?"

Rory flashed a little grin, remembering the bath she'd given him yesterday. She had apologized a couple more times about it and they were cool.

Grams liked the idea. "That would be grand. Why don't you all come with us?"

"Can we, Mom?" Rory asked. He didn't look at Eddie.

"Sounds like a splendid idea," she replied.

The buffet was set up at one end of the pool – all cold meats, salads, and fruit, with an ice sculpture of a dolphin melting in the middle. They ate at a table near the railing, where they could watch people walk by on one side and see the waves shimmering off the horizon on the other. A bank of dark clouds was rolling in from the east and the air was a bit chilly. While they ate, Rory sat beside Lucy, half listening to her babble and also keeping an ear on the adults, hoping his mother wouldn't embarrass him.

"Eddie and I met six months ago," Claire was telling Grams. "I'd been divorced from Rory's father for over a year. It was time to move on."

Grams nodded. "Divorce is hard on the whole family."

"Does Lucy live with you, Mrs. Donnelly?" Eddie asked.

"No. Her family lives in Cambridge. I'm down on the Cape," Grams explained. "She has four boisterous brothers and two very busy parents."

"Excuse me," Lucy interrupted. "I'm right here."

"You needn't point that out, my girl. Your presence is felt wherever you go." Grams laughed.

"You two seem to get along so well," Claire said. "It's nice to see that."

"Grams and me always –" Lucy began, and then suddenly leaned over the table towards the deck. "Hi, Michel!"

she called to a passing man in *Sea Lion* crew shirt and shorts. The young man turned and waved.

"Hi, Lucy. You having fun?" he replied, as he walked by.

"That's the diving instructor I was telling you about, Grams. We did snorkeling this morning and he's going to teach me how to use respirators," she explained. "Oh, there goes the drummer from the rock band that plays at the disco bar. I met him last night." She waved as she caught his eye. He waved back.

Rory admired her pluck. She was so fearless. He would never wave and say hi to anybody. He barely made eye contact with adults and didn't think they would even remember him. But Lucy was so up front about everything that it made him feel part of something special just to be near her.

"She'll go on like this all day," Grams told them. "Give her an hour anywhere and she'll know everyone."

"Will not," Lucy protested, but she wasn't very convincing. "I just like to know who's around, that's all."

"What have you folks planned for the afternoon?" Grams asked.

"Not much," Claire admitted. "Frankly, all these scheduled activities tire me out just hearing about them."

"I know what you mean."

"Might just stay here," Eddie added. "This is as good a spot as any."

"Can Lucy and I go?" Rory blurted out.

"You going to meet Judy and the other kids?" Claire laughed and looked at her watch. "It's almost 0100."

"Not if I can help it," Rory answered.

"Judy?" Lucy asked. "Oh, you mean, the junior cruise queen?"

"Well, have fun," Claire said.

The two kids jumped up with their sodas.

"Be back for supper," Eddie warned.

"Keep Lucy from sinking the ship, would you, Rory?" Grams added.

"I'll keep her from shenanigans," Rory promised, sure it was the right word.

Grams gave him a queer look and smiled. "That's good. Steer clear of them shenanigans."

Claire rolled her eyes as they headed off. . . .

As soon as they were out of earshot, Rory said, "Wait till you hear! I found a picture of Mr. Morgan on my computer."

"No way!" Lucy squealed. "Where?"

Rory spilled everything. He told her about his scrapbook and the flash card guessing game, the pictures of *Titanic* survivors, right up to the trip to the engine rooms that morning. He got so excited that everything came out all jumbled up.

"Super cool! Where's the picture?"

"It's on my laptop in my cabin. I'll show you later."

"You don't think he's a ghost, do you?" she said in spooky tones, while wiggling her fingers in the air around her head. "That would make him, like, eighty, for the past hundred years."

They stopped at the railing and looked straight down at the lifeboats, three decks below them. Rory tried to sound casual. "My mom thinks the picture is probably somebody who looks like him. Maybe his father or grandfather. You know, real look-alikes." He tried to tell Lucy about Morgan and the crewman. The blank haunted look on the crewman's face gave him a bad feeling.

"Did you ask old Morg about it?" Lucy said.

Rory looked at his feet.

"You are, like, so KFC, Rory Dugan." She clucked like a chicken. "We'll have to do something about that one of these days. Meantime, we need to prove he's a ghost."

"How? Come right out and ask him?"

Lucy crumpled her soda cup and let it fall on top of a lifeboat. He did the same. They took longer to hit than he expected.

"Something like that," she said.

"'Excuse me, my friend and I are wondering if you're a ghost?'"

"That sounds good. But try and sound a bit more dejected."

"What if he turns mean on us?"

"You said he's nice."

"Not all the time. Besides, snakes seem nice, too, until you poke 'em with a stick."

Lucy snorted and headed off.

This was bad news. There were only two ways with Lucy: lots of fun and lots of trouble.

"Come on, fraidy-cat. Let's go," she called. And that was that. All he could do was scramble to catch up.

"Remember what happened the last time you ran off without a plan?"

"We're smarter now. More experienced."

"Wouldn't it be better if we watch him to see if he does any ghosty things?" Rory asked.

"Like what? See if he walks through walls, or turns invisible?"

"I could get my mom's camera and take a picture," he suggested hopefully. "I heard you can't take pictures of ghosts. Wouldn't that be proof?"

But Lucy wasn't listening. She was studying a deck map on the wall beside the elevator. A shadow crossed the sky and he looked up to see that the sun was now completely covered by the clouds, and the seas were starting to get a bit choppy. He hoped it wasn't a bad sign.

Over the next hour they clambered up and down stairs, through passages, searching the promenade, the lobby, three lounges, and even the gymnasium. Mr. Morgan was in none of those places. Rory knew that already. He was fairly sure he could find him if he wanted to. But he didn't tell Lucy. In fact, when he closed his eyes and thought about it, he felt he could picture exactly where the old man was. . . .

At one point they had to duck into a hairdresser's while Judy went by with some kids. "I bet they're off to have some fun with a capital PH," Lucy said. Then she tried to talk Rory into getting his hair spiked to make Eddie mad. He didn't bite.

Finally, they found themselves back on the promenade, watching the sea start to crest with whitecaps. Rough weather was moving in and the whole ship was rocking gently. It felt like riding over hilly roads in a big car. Rory liked it.

A voice boomed over the intercom system. "This is Captain Levesque. A minor squall has turned into our path. The seas may be a little rough and we'll be getting some rain for the next few hours. Folks might want to stay indoors for a while."

Rory wanted front row seats to this. "Come on! Let's go watch from the bow," he said and sped off. Lucy followed him up the three flights of stairs, right to Rory's favorite spot on the foredeck. It was deserted. Rain tapped on their faces and hands as they gripped the bow rail on the edge of a fifty-foot drop to the rolling ocean below. They watched breathlessly as big waves tumbled towards the ship and crashed into the hull. As the *Sea Lion* pitched and rolled, they felt the deck rise and fall right under their feet. The little sailboat ride with his father was no comparison to this. The sea was coming at them from all sides, throwing cold rain and wind in their faces. Water fogged his glasses so much, he could hardly see. But the waves never knocked either of them down.

Right in the middle of the pitching, Rory started to feel strange – hot and itchy, almost giddy even. His foggy vision cleared and he looked around as if he were seeing something that wasn't there.

He found himself clutching the rail on the deck of a different ship, a wooden ship, as she broached to the wind in some ghost storm. She was tipped so far over that the water was nearly up to the railing and the deck was on a forty-five degree slant. Panic raced through him as he leaned way back to keep from toppling right over the side and into the churning sea.

"Save yourself. Save yourself!" he muttered in a guttural voice that didn't sound like his own.

"Rory!" called a voice in the distance. "Rory! Are you alright?"

He blinked a few times and saw a girl's face through the water drops on his glasses. He recognized her. *Lucy, my new friend.* He smiled. She smiled back. She seemed very relieved.

"You looked like you were going to jump overboard, or something," she said, while gripping his shoulders. "Let's go inside." He nodded and she pulled his hands off the railing and led him away. They were both shivering from the cold and soaked to the bone, with water dripping down their faces and necks.

Warm air hit them and the spell broke.

"You weirded me out there for a sec," she said. "Are you okay?"

"*Uh* . . . y-y-yeah. I'm f-fine," he replied through chattering teeth.

"I'm taking you back to your cabin."

"S-S-Stateroom," he said.

"Yeah. That, too."

As they headed down to Rory's stateroom, Lucy pointed to all the vomit bags that were tied to the railing every couple of feet along the halls, and tried to make jokes to cheer Rory up. It didn't have much effect. This vision didn't fade away as the others had.

"Listen," he said, stopping just outside his stateroom. "We've got to look some stuff up on my computer. Can you hang around?"

"Sure thing. You've got to tell me what's going on, though."

"Okay." They squished into his stateroom to find his mother waiting for him. The air smelled of puke. They could hear Eddie groaning on the bed with every roll of the ship. Rory could see by the look on his mother's face that it was lecture time. But as soon as she noticed Lucy behind him, also dripping water all over the floor, she smiled thinly. Lucy and Rory looked at each other and crinkled their noses.

"You're both soaked," Claire observed sharply. "Get out of those wet things right away, or you'll catch cold. You best go back to your cabin and change, Lucy. I expect your grandmother will be worried that you stayed out in this bad weather."

"Grams knows I'm okay," Lucy assured her with a wave of a hand. "Rory promised to show me something on his computer." She smiled her most disarming elfish smile, the one that had worked so well on Officer Bergeron the day before.

Rory knew it was wasted. His mom was made of sterner stuff than any sailor. "Mr. Farentino isn't feeling well," she explained. "Perhaps later would be better."

"We could go to my cabin," Lucy suggested.

Encouraged by her persistence, Rory joined in. "I can change right away and we'll be out of your hair until supper," he blurted, trying out his biggest goofy smile on her. Claire glanced over her shoulder at the curtain drawn in front of the bed, where they could hear Eddie being seasick again. She didn't look all that good, either, Rory realized. "You probably want quiet anyway," he added.

"Grams won't mind us there," Lucy said, pointing at the phone. "I can even call and make sure."

Before Claire could make up her mind, Rory handed Lucy the phone, then mopped up the puddles with a couple of towels. He picked out a dry shirt and jeans and squeezed into the bathroom to change.

Through the door he could hear Lucy hang up the phone and his mother say, "We look about the same size. You can wear these to get back to your room." Rory grinned from ear to ear. *Lucy is something else.*

"Thanks," he heard her answer and, when he came out, she was already changed into his mom's gym shorts and top. The last few rolls of the ship had Claire lurching off to join Eddie in the sickbed. He grabbed his computer and he and Lucy headed for Deck 5. When they got to Lucy's cabin, Grams wasn't there.

"Did she say she was going out?" Rory asked.

"*Nah*. No one answered. I made up that conversation with her." Lucy giggled. "Relax," she said in response to his surprised look. "You really have to learn how to lie to your parents."

Proof

"**S**ee? That's him." Rory pointed at the picture of Mr. Morgan and the Lowreys on his computer. Ever since he'd been blown around the foredeck, he'd been dying to boot up and look at this picture again. He stared into the dark eyes of the man in the back row, while he told Lucy about the strange vision he'd just had.

They were sitting together on the small sofa in her stateroom. The choppy seas outside rocked the ship and pelted the sliding glass doors with spray. Rory and Lucy didn't mind. The computer between them and steaming mugs of room service hot chocolate on the floor, they were content and he felt safe.

"So what do we do next?" Lucy asked. "I mean, if all this weird stuff you're going through is true, what does it mean?"

"Last night, I ran a check on the *Titanic* passenger manifest to find Morgan and his name wasn't there," Rory said. "I tried different spellings, too."

"What's a manifest?" Lucy asked.

"It's what they call the passenger list." He started tapping keys.

"Your mom doesn't like me, does she?"

That came out of nowhere, Rory thought. "It's their honeymoon," he explained. "They dragged me along on this trip thinking it'll make us a happy family, or something. It's so lame."

"I know what you mean. My folks are always trying to organize a 'family' night. It never works," she replied. "So, where do we find a manifest?"

"I had it last night, so I know it's here somewhere." He kept punching keys and searching the screen. "This computer has a huge hard drive and a ton of web pages. Sometimes I forget where things are."

"You're pretty smart with this thing."

That pleased him. "My dad and I downloaded these sites off the Internet. He taught me how to set up my own, too. My dad's great."

"He seems pretty sick."

That hurt. "That's Eddie, my new *step*father."

"Oh, right . . . their honeymoon."

"I was supposed to stay with Dad, but something came up. He owns a computer company in Chicago."

"Sounds like you'd rather live there."

"Well, Eddie is a pain and Mom is always getting on my case about being depressed, or something."

"Most divorced kids I know get an easier deal at their dad's."

"He doesn't boss me, if that's what you mean."

"Something like that. Fiona says her dad just buys her stuff all the time."

"Mine, too," he agreed. "Are your parents divorced?"

"No," Lucy said. Then she added, "Not yet, anyway. I guess it's normal for everybody to get divorced."

"Yeah," he agreed. *But if it's so normal, why does it hurt so much?*

The browser downloaded a long list of names that could be clicked on. "Here it comes." He scrolled to the *M*'s. "See. No Morgan."

"Is that everyone?" Lucy took a sip of her hot chocolate.

"Including the crew."

She thought for a second. "What if Morgan isn't his real name? Or maybe it's his first name."

"Hey, neat idea!" Rory gave a high five. "You're pretty smart, too," he said, and tried to think of a way to do a search. He scrolled back up to the top name. The only real proof would be a picture. "Rats," he groaned. "We'll have to go through every single passenger on this list and hope there's a picture of him."

"So?"

"There are almost two thousand names. It could take forever."

"Really?" Lucy was amazed. "You have pictures of everybody who was on the *Titanic?*"

"Almost. Practically all the survivors were photographed by the newspapers, after they were rescued. Like the one I showed you. Most of those pictures are here. The pictures of the people who died are taken from earlier times."

"You did all that?" She was impressed.

"*Nah.*" Rory wished he had. "I only downloaded it."

He hoped they would find something. He wanted so badly to understand Mr. Morgan. The old man had gotten inside him and was trying to tell him something.

They both leaned forward. Rory clicked on the first name. It wasn't him. He went back and clicked the next. No luck. After about twenty, they sat back.

"I see what you mean." Lucy sighed.

Rory kept on clicking while they drank hot chocolate and talked. Lucy asked him about school and his life in Kansas. They compared stories about the teachers and subjects they were taking. It was fun. Then he told her what he thought of some of the other kids in his class and talked about the chat rooms he hung out in on the Internet.

"Don't you have any friends?" she asked.

"I stick to myself," he answered defensively, and wondered for the first time in a long time why he was always by himself these days. He'd forgotten what it was like to hang out with a friend.

"That must be boring."

"Well, there's this geek they call Weiner that I trade software with. And I know a couple of guys who always talk about *Star Wars*. Usually, I read lots. I don't know. It's okay."

"That's so different from me. Me and my posse – that's Sarah, Chloe, Margarete, and Fiona – all go to Harvard Square and window-shop and get sodas and meet guys. Most times my parents don't even know I go. They think I vamp it around the house after school. But I'd go totally Friday the 13th if I stayed home. Even one day."

"Does sound like fun," Rory agreed. *But no one ever invites me to go anywhere.* "Reading isn't so bad. There's a lot of cool stories in books. I get lost in them. Movies, too," he added.

Lucy had to disagree. "I hate being alone. It's like computers. I can never get the hang of them because you've got to work alone so much."

He had to admit being with Lucy was giving him doubts about his solitude. But it was his world and it was safe.

"Got any malls around you?" she asked.

"By bus. Oh, we do have Willards."

"Willards? Sounds like a creepy movie."

"It's this great corner store. They have everything. Models, comics, computer games, trains even. And a candy wall that'd leave you speechless. The whole store smells great."

"I could get into that."

"The used comic books are the best," he continued, hardly noticing that he was the one doing the babbling. "You can shuffle through them for hours and pick what you want. I get five for a dollar and then sell them back at half-price, so I can buy more!"

"That sounds pretty cool," she said.

He talked on about other things for a while, and then they sat quietly watching picture after picture of strangers in long dresses and fancy suits, piled hairdos, and bushy mustaches flash across the screen.

"That's the kind of suit Mr. Morgan is wearing," Rory said. "And it's weird because he's had the same one on since he came aboard."

"Really? I've only seen him a couple of times. Maybe he has several identical ones," she suggested.

After they had gone through two hundred and thirty files and were only up to the letter *H*, Rory wondered for the millionth time if they should give up for a while. He kept telling himself, *just one more.* . . . His mouse hand was getting sore as he clicked on the next name: Hewett. A picture of an elderly couple appeared.

"It's him!" Rory cried, and a shiver ran up his back. Both kids jumped and nearly knocked the computer on the floor.

"No way!" Lucy cheered. "Let me see again!"

They looked again. Posing in a similar suit and tie, Morgan sat beside an old woman wearing a high-collared flower-patterned dress. There was no mistaking him as anyone but the man who was traveling on the *Sea Lion*.

"It's him alright." Rory was confident. "But, that isn't the lady who was in the picture behind the Lowreys."

"This is so cool!" Lucy exclaimed.

Now that they had found it, Rory wasn't so sure. He was half hoping there would be a more ordinary explanation. Finding this picture complicated things. It may have answered the question of who Morgan was, but it raised an even bigger and scarier question. *Why is he here?*

"He really was on the *Titanic!*" Lucy's spooked voice whispered as though it just sank in. "What do you think it means?" She squeezed Rory's arm.

"It means I'm scared," Rory answered.

The page finished downloading onto his screen. Rory read aloud: "Mr. and Mrs. *Morgan* Hewett, aged 76 and 78, traveled in second class." He shuddered, not daring to believe it. "They lived in New York and were returning from Europe. Morgan Hewett was a naval lieutenant in the Union Army during the Civil War. After the war, he worked for the navy as an engineer and later helped form the Office of Naval Intelligence. The Hewetts had four children."

"And look," Lucy pointed further down the page. "It says Olivia Hewett died on the *Titanic*." Her grip was starting to hurt Rory's arm. "But it doesn't say what happened to him. Just that he survived. The date and cause of his death are unknown."

"This gives me the creeps. There's a ghost haunting this ship! What do you think he wants?"

They looked at each other and the color drained from their faces as they imagined answers to that question. Rory thought about the vision of the sinking ship he'd had on deck.

Something scraped the door!

"AAAAAAH!" both of them screamed, and their heads smacked together in a scramble to jump up. *"Oww!"* they groaned, clutching their foreheads and flopping back on the sofa.

It was Grams.

Lucy and Rory sighed with relief.

"What are you two up to?" she demanded from the doorway, the key card in her hand.

Rubbing their heads, they exchanged guilty looks.

Grams shook her head and laughed. "Nice to see you, Rory," she said. "It's dress-up night in the dining room, young lady, and you have to get ready."

"Is it supper time already?" Lucy cried. "We're in the middle of something."

"Yes, it is, and we have a cocktail party to attend before dinner. Chop-chop."

"Can Rory come with us?"

"Not this time," Grams replied. "We're to dine at the captain's table and it's by invitation only."

Lucy got up reluctantly and started looking for clothes. She was still wearing his mother's shorts. Grams went into the bathroom.

"Let's keep this quiet for now, okay?" Lucy whispered. "At least until we have time to come up with a plan."

"You're really eating at the captain's table?" Rory was envious.

"I guess. I forgot about it."

"Maybe you should tell him what we found out," he suggested.

She shook her head. "Not yet. Let's keep it P.I. for a while."

"P.I.?"

"Private Information."

Rory wanted to object, but Grams came out and he held his thought. He wasn't so sure they should stay quiet. Morgan Hewett was dangerous. Probably more dangerous than he could ever imagine.

"How are you surviving the rough seas?" Grams asked him.

"*Huh?*" Rory replied, still trying to think straight. "Oh, my mother and stepfather are sick, but I'm okay."

"That's too bad for them."

"I know what I'll wear," Lucy announced and picked something off the floor.

"You'll wear the dress," Grams told her. "And no nonsense."

Lucy glared sourly at her. "I brought my own clothes, you know. I don't need to wear that junior miss crap."

"It would never do to have you stumbling to the captain's table looking like a Martian."

"I'd rather eat with Martians," she said.

"I'd love to sit at the captain's table," Rory said.

Lucy stuck her finger down her throat and made gagging noises.

"That's none too ladylike, now, is it?" Grams said. "I hope you don't do that at table."

"I better go," Rory said, and headed for the door with his computer tucked under his arm.

"See you later, Ror!" Lucy called after him.

Line of Fire

The dining room was buzzing with hundreds of people dressed in evening gowns and tuxedos. At one end was a bandstand, with a small jazz band churning out boring old tunes that all sounded the same to Rory. In the center hung a huge crystal chandelier that cast glimmers of light and color all over the room. Right underneath it was the captain's table, elevated slightly on a platform so everyone could see the captain's honored guests each evening. Tonight it was Lucy and Grams, among a dozen others.

Everyone was having fun. Everyone except Rory. At his table were the same people they ate with every night: Mr. and Mrs. Boxner from Detroit; the von Heflens, an elderly couple traveling to visit relatives in Florida; and a French guy named Claude, who smelled like garlic. As usual, Eddie griped about the food and bragged about his used cars in Kansas. The only good part was that he still looked a little green and more uncomfortable in his suit and tie than Rory did.

Rory thought the food was good. That night was roast chicken and mashed potatoes and some popover thingies he'd never heard of but ate as many as his mom would let him. All through dinner he squirmed and tugged at the geeky suit he had to wear, while keeping a watchful eye on the captain's table. He had seen Lucy come in, wearing a knee-length blue dress that he thought was pretty. From where he sat he could watch her yakking away, squeezed between two ship's officers. *She's fearless. She can fit in anywhere and get along with anyone.* In his imagination Rory believed he could talk to strangers too, but as soon as a real situation came up he just froze.

All their talk that afternoon about school and friends had confused him. It had brought up memories of what a different life he'd had before his dad left . . . before Ian died. He had been bolder, willing to try new things and talk to people. He had lots of friends. He even remembered what a great little brother Ian had been and how close they were. That was dangerous because it hurt the most. Allowing himself to miss Ian only made him feel worse about what happened and how he should have saved him. And that always brought him back to the same place: *it's my fault.*

"Dinner's over, Rory. Why don't you go up and say hello to Lucy and Abigail?" Claire suggested, as she wiped a wine stain off her blouse. "I'm sure they would be happy to introduce you to Captain Levesque. You look like you've been pining to all through dinner."

"It's obvious that you'd love to go," said Mr. von Heflen, sipping his brandy. "You've been staring up there since you sat down."

"I wouldn't know what to say," he replied sullenly. The last thing he wanted to do was buzz around the captain's table uninvited. At the same time, he wished he could go up and grab Lucy, so they could get out of there. He couldn't explain why, but he had an uncontrollable urge to find Morgan. It was hard to resist, like wanting to go look in the closet where the Christmas presents are hidden, even though you shouldn't.

"Are you kidding?" Eddie joked. "You probably know more about the ship than the captain does."

Rory glowered. *This could get messy if they make me go,* he thought. Then he had an idea. "Okay, I'll go. But let me pick when."

"Attaboy," Eddie said. "Oh, I almost forgot. Here." He pulled something out of his pocket and put it down in front of Rory. "I picked this up at the museum for you this afternoon." It was a small book on the construction of ocean liners.

Rory flipped through it a couple of times. It was kind of neat, much as he hated to admit it. "Thanks," he said. That made his mother smile.

Keeping his eye on the captain's table while he looked at the book, he saw his break. "I'm going right now," he announced, and was off like a shot. Once out of sight of his parents, he veered off to intercept Lucy on her way to the bathroom.

"Hey, Ror," she said, a bit surprised to see him there.

"Hi. Want to help me find Morgan Hewett right now?" he asked. "Can you get away?"

"I was hoping something would save me from this snorefest. I haven't seen anyone under three hundred years old all night. Give me five mins," she replied, and turned back to her table.

"I'll meet you outside in the reception room," he called.

Careful to stay out of sight of his parents, Rory snuck out and waited in the anteroom that adjoined the dining room. It was an open hall with red carpets, plush chairs, and a big leather bar at one end. The only people there were the bartenders and a few passengers walking through from dinner. Rory sank into a huge red chair and tried to look invisible, in case anyone from his table walked by.

He closed his eyes and could almost see an image of Morgan down on the engineering deck. He could see him surrounded by machinery, arguing with a bunch of men. The vision was so strong that it made him jump.

"What do you think of this wimpy dress Grams made me wear?" Lucy asked, with an exaggerated curtsy. "I swear, she thinks I'm still six."

"*Huh?*" Rory's head snapped up.

"You weirding out on me again?" she asked.

"No. I'm okay," he replied and looked at her dress. "I kind of like it," he said sheepishly, "but I'm not doing much better." He flicked his red bow tie.

"You do look like someone else dressed you," she said, looking him over. "So what's the plan?"

"I've got a feeling that Morgan is in trouble."

"So?"

"I can't explain why. But I think the ship may be in danger." That was the first time he'd put it that way and it made sense. Like several thoughts coming together and forming a new idea.

"Because of him?" Lucy asked.

Rory shrugged. "I'm sure he's the one making me feel so strange and have all those weird visions."

"Where to?"

"Deck 15," he said confidently.

"Good enough for me. But we better not stay too long. I told Grams I was going up to the disco. If we get in trouble downstairs, she'll kill me."

Off they went, this time with Rory leading and Lucy taking her cues from him. Just outside the anteroom, he located the crew door. When no one was looking, he clicked open the tiny latch, and slipped out of sight.

"You've been holding out on me," she said lightheart-edly, and squeezed in behind him.

"I watched Morgan go in one of these yesterday," he explained, as she shut the door behind her.

Rory lead the way down. They ignored the waiters they met, but hid when they saw other crew members coming. After a while, and a few more stairways, they stopped on a deck that was laid out differently from any Rory had seen so far. He knew somehow that this was it, as if he had been there before.

There were no doors, rooms, or corridors. It was a well-lit cavern of causeways and steel grate flooring that wound around between huge tanks, weird-looking contraptions, and noisy machinery. Massive white painted pipes ran overhead, with faucets and levers suspended from them. The air was hot and steamy, and everything was smeared with grease. The pounding of the ship's great engines belted right in their ears.

Looking over his shoulder, Rory saw two men coming up and yanked Lucy into a corner just in time. He couldn't see them, but the voices were so close that he thought he could reach out and trip them as they went by. After they passed, Lucy peeked out and signaled that the coast was clear. "Where are we going?" she asked, as loudly as she dared.

"I'm not sure." His vision of where to find Morgan was getting stronger. He also sensed that the old man was in danger. "Let's try down there."

They prowled around the causeways, keeping a sharp lookout in all directions. Lucy jabbed him in the side and pointed. "There's someone over there! They're coming this way."

Rory heard them before he saw them: three men yelling over the engine noise at the far end of a ramp.

"Over here!" He grabbed Lucy's arm. They crammed close together, crouching between two churning machines that looked like whiskey stills. It was so steamy that he had to wipe off his glasses. He felt a bit scared but when he looked at Lucy, sweating, her eyes sparkling with excitement and her pointy smile, he figured they were okay. She didn't even notice that her new dress was smeared with grease. His jacket was taking a beating, too.

The men stopped in an open space nearby and pointed at some gauges on the wall. They spoke loudly to each other. Rory couldn't catch what they said because of the other noises around him. Suddenly, the tone got angry.

Rory wiped a sweaty hand across his face and risked a peep around the drum. There were four men there now. Two were tall stringy guys in greasy overalls and T-shirts, the third was an older guy in a white officer's uniform, with no hair and a face like a bulldog. They were yelling at the fourth guy. He was old and – .

"It's Morgan!" Rory whispered hoarsely. "And he's mad." Red in the face from yelling, he was waving some papers he clutched in his fist and pointing at the same gauges on the wall.

"Let me see!" Lucy exclaimed, and pulled Rory away to get a look. She sat back down beside him. "They're steamed. What do you figure he did?"

"We're not close enough to hear anything."

"I bet we can if we get closer to the other side of this vat." She pointed at the big machine blocking their way. "If one of us could squeeze between these two drums, I bet we'd hear them."

"It looks too tight," Rory observed.

"I don't think I could make it," she whispered, "but you're smaller than me."

"I'll try." Rory tore off his jacket and started wriggling in between the two drums. It was hot and very tight. When he was halfway through, something caught. He heard his pants tear. *Not only am I going to die here, but Mom is going to kill me for ruining this stupid suit.* He stretched until he thought something would snap inside him. It was no use. He couldn't quite reach the lip of the metal frame. *I'm stuck for good.* "Pull me back!" he whispered over his shoulder. "Quick!"

Suddenly, he felt a familiar foot on his butt pushing him! *She's going to get me stuck in here for keeps!* "NO! Puuuulllll!"

Lucy kept on pushing. He had no choice but to try and reach for the frame again. With every muscle sore and straining to the limit, he managed to catch the tips of his fingers over the edge of a steel plate that had some warm slime smeared all over it. He hoped it was only grease as his fingers squished into it, and he pulled with all the strength he could find. Lucy's painful jabs in his rear got him the rest of the way, but it was like being squeezed between the railings of a fence. His guts hurt and he was sure he'd have bruises on his butt. But he was through.

He turned around and gave Lucy a dirty look. She grinned her elfish grin, gave him the thumbs-up, and waved her foot. Shaking his head, he crawled carefully to the edge and peeked around. He had to admit it was a perfect view as he rubbed his sore belly.

"Are you deaf? I told you fifteen times already," Morgan bellowed at one of the skinny workmen, who looked twice his size. "You've got a hydraulics problem."

"How would you know?" asked the other thin one, marking his words with a prod into Morgan's arm.

"Check the system," Morgan snapped.

"If you don't stay on the passenger decks," yelled the bulldog in the white uniform, "I'll have you confined." His angry red face gave Rory the shivers. But Morgan didn't flinch. He just yelled back.

To Rory's amazement, the whole scene looked just as he had envisioned it back in the dining room. *How can this be? I've never been here!* Then it got stranger. Morgan looked over Officer Bulldog's shoulder and straight into Rory's eyes! It jolted him like putting a knife in a wall socket. A knowing smile creased the old man's lips, as if Rory was expected. Rory couldn't tear his eyes away. *He knew we were coming. But how?*

"You call the captain. Then we'll see." Morgan shook his walking stick at the bulldog-faced officer.

"I won't bother the captain with the likes of you," the officer bellowed back. He snatched the stick from the old man's hand.

"You dog-robber!" Morgan cursed, his gravelly voice booming over the loud machinery. "Men lose their lives due to incompetent pencil pushers the likes of you!"

"Call security," the bulldog barked to one of the other men. The man nodded silently and backed away towards an intercom on the wall.

The tension was thicker than the steamy air. Rory could feel the weight of it. Like a storm cloud, it had to break. Sure enough, with a signal from the bulldog, the other workman grabbed Morgan's arms from behind. He strained so hard to free himself that the veins on his neck stood out like knotted rope. But he couldn't.

Rory felt himself struggling, too. He twitched and squirmed like he was having a seizure. When Morgan stopped fighting, so did he.

"I was a naval officer before your grandfather could spit up oatmeal," Morgan hissed, goading the bulldog into a fight. "Time was when I'd have a flink like you drummed out of the service!"

"Well, this ain't the navy," the bulldog replied, and shoved Morgan backwards with the tip of the cane into the guy who was holding him. It set them off balance and Morgan broke free. He raised his fists like claws, ready to strike. The bulldog took a swing with his fist, but Morgan swayed out of reach.

Rory could feel his own arm jerk up, as if to fend off the punch. Then, almost like being pulled on strings, he jumped out of his hiding place and planted himself between Morgan and Officer Bulldog. The workmen jumped back. Morgan stood his ground. For a second, Rory felt a rush of cold air chill the sweat he was drenched in. He knew now that this was a signal of something that he didn't yet understand.

"Grandfather!" he heard himself say, his voice shaking. He looked up at Morgan. "You know you shouldn't be out . . . after you take your medication." His hands were as unsteady as his voice.

"Rory!" Morgan said, trying to sound surprised.

They all stared. Out of the corner of his eye, Rory caught Lucy's astonished expression from her hiding place. He looked pleadingly into the old man's eyes for some direction and was met by a sly grin and a wink.

"Now, child, I'll be alright." Morgan began his feeble act. "Doc said I would only hallucinate if there were loud noises." He spoke much quieter now and put on his goofy expression, with his teeth sticking out.

"Who are you?" the bulldog demanded.

Rory took Morgan's clammy hand. "I'm sorry if Grandpa caused any trouble. He must have had one of his spells," he said, his heart beating wildly, his throat dry as ashes. The cold air had gone and the heat was making him swoon. "He's ill and should be in bed. The pills always do this."

"What happened to your clothes, boy?" one of the others asked. He tugged on Rory's grease-stained red bow tie.

"I came looking for Grandpa," Rory replied, hardly knowing where the words came from. "I didn't have time to change."

"Where are we anyway?" Morgan asked, in a bewildered weak voice. "This isn't the dining room, is it?" He looked straight at the men and sounded like a patient in a nursing home. "I guess we'll need a table for two."

The men frowned and scratched their heads. Morgan blinked and looked like a puff of air would blow him down.

"This man says he used to be in the navy. Is that true?" Officer Bulldog demanded.

"Has he been telling you about engine problems?" Rory asked.

"Yes," he replied, suspiciously.

Rory was amazed. *It really does worry people if they think you're crazy.* "Please let me take him back to bed. I promise we'll make sure he stays out of trouble."

"When we get to Richmond," Morgan declared, "I'll see that you are all stripped of rank and court-martialed."

That did it. "Take him back to his stateroom, boy, and be sure he stays there," Bulldog finally decided. "Mind you, if I see either of you down here again, you'll be fined and put off this ship at the first port!"

Rory looked over to Lucy. She held a finger to her lips and shooed him off. *Maybe she knows best.* He and Morgan were escorted to the elevator and sent on their way.

"That was brave," Morgan chuckled, as the car lifted them to safety.

Rory couldn't explain it, but something had pulled him out of hiding like a vacuum cleaner sucking up dust. It had even led him down there in the first place. Looking at Morgan, he wondered if he knew what was going on. Suddenly, Rory felt very tired and wanted to sleep. "We bluejackets should look after each other" was all he could think to say.

The old man laid a gentle hand on his shoulder. "That we should. I suggest you get below and slip out of those clothes before your parents find out what you've done to them. You look as though you dismantled a steam engine."

Rory looked at himself. *Wow! My whole suit is ruined.* He'd lost his jacket, his shirt was covered in grease, and his pants were shredded down one side. "Why were you yelling at those men?" He tried to wipe the smears off his glasses.

"Good question," Morgan replied, doing the same with his specs. "But let's save all that for tomorrow. There is still time. Besides," he added, as he stepped off the elevator on Deck 10, "you have to go back and rescue the young lady."

The doors closed, leaving Rory alone and as baffled as ever. He got off at Deck 11 and retraced his steps downstairs, looking for Lucy. He didn't have to go far.

One flight down, he met her coming up. Her dress was in better shape than his suit, but not much. A wonderful smile lit up her dirty face.

"Hey, Ror!" she laughed. "That was a wicked stunt you pulled. I didn't hear half of it, but I thought you were going to get your block knocked off."

"I don't know what happened. I just –"

"You sure did," she agreed, as they climbed the stairs together, poking each other to relieve their tension.

Teaming Up with Trouble

Rory did get back to the cabin before his mother. It was almost nine o'clock. He hid his tattered clothes under sofa cushions and took a quick shower. He felt better with all the dirt cleaned off. Back in jeans and short sleeves, he decided to go find his mom so she wouldn't be suspicious of his disappearing after supper. *What a day! What's going to happen next?* He lay down on his bed to catch his breath and fell asleep.

He woke up and stretched. The nap had felt good. *Better go find Mom,* he thought, still feeling groggy. As his head cleared, he slipped on his glasses and looked at his watch. It was 8:15. *How can it be forty-five minutes earlier?* He noticed he was wearing pajamas. Then it dawned. *It's morning!*

He sat bolt upright, trying to think. *I remember going below to rescue Morgan, and then talking to Lucy before we split up for the night. Right! Then I lay down for a couple of minutes. Oh, rats! If it's the morning, I'm supposed to meet Lucy on the foredeck at nine.*

He and Lucy had decided that even after seeing Morgan with the crewmen, they didn't know much more about him than they had before supper. Today they were going to get some answers. *An* answer really, to one important question. *Why is this ghost on the ship?*

After a quick trip to the bathroom, Rory charted the ship's position at about 1000 miles west of Spain. It was another thousand to Newfoundland, the nearest civilized coast. He peeped around the curtain to see who else was up. Eddie was gone and his mom was propped up in bed, reading a magazine with a cup of coffee under her nose. *She'll let me go, I know it.*

"There you are sleepyhead," she yawned.

"Hi, Mom."

"We wondered if you would ever get up."

Rory sat on the end of his mom's bed. He still felt groggy.

"What did you do after supper?" she asked. "You were fast asleep in your clothes when we got back."

"Me and Lucy went to play some video games and stuff," he lied. *Lucy is right, it's not that hard to do.* "I was going to find you afterwards, but must have dozed off."

"We were feeling better, so we saw a play at the theater. You would have loved it. It was very funny."

Rory wanted badly to tell her about Morgan and the strange feelings that had begun to haunt him. He knew he had to tell her, but the words just wouldn't come out. Something told him that if he didn't – or couldn't – spill it all now, he wouldn't get another chance. But the more he tried to focus, the foggier it all seemed to get. It became so muddied and confusing, in fact, that he could hardly lay his hands on a single word or clear thought. They just balled up in his throat and made it hard to breathe.

But if he didn't try to speak, he got a better picture, like shards of a broken mirror pieced together to reflect a single image. Something frightening was happening on this ship, and inside of him – something beyond his control.

"Rory?" she asked. "You look pale. Is everything alright?"

Just tell her, he said to himself. *Say anything.* But he couldn't.

The door clicked. Eddie was back.

"Hi, gang," he said. He dropped the ship's newsletter, *Ships Ahoy!,* on the bed and kicked off his shoes.

"Hi, dear," Claire said.

"According to the blab, there's all sorts of things to do today. Anything from Kabuki napkin-folding to dodging automatic weapon fire." Eddie chuckled and rolled onto the bed beside his wife. It created a ripple effect that sloshed his mom's coffee and almost toppled Rory off the end.

"Eddie!" she cried. "Be careful." She threw a pillow over the spill and turned to Rory. "What did you want to tell me, Rory?"

"Nothing," he replied.

"Y'alright there, sport?" Eddie asked. He started leafing through the newsletter without looking up. "Let's see here. I saw something I thought you'd like, hon."

"Oh? What?"

Rory got dressed in shorts and sneakers and sat by the porthole, looking out to sea. The day was sunny and the ocean calm. *I have to meet Lucy in ten minutes. How do I get away?* He listened absently as Eddie and his mom made plans.

"Lucy and I want to meet at nine," he blurted. "Can I go?"

Both adults fell silent. A long second passed while Rory felt their scrutiny burn through him. *Here's where the know-it-all Poundcake butts in.* He waited for the axe to fall.

"Okay," said Mom.

"See you," said Eddie.

They went back to circling items in the newsletter.

Rory frowned, wondering if this was a joke. But only for a split second. He grabbed the picture of the Hewetts that he had printed for Lucy and was gone. "Bye."

"Drop in now and then to let us know what's up," Claire added, as the door closed behind him.

Up on the foredeck, the air was crisp. Rory leaned on the railing, looking out to sea, and bit into a cheese Danish from the breakfast buffet. The frustration and edgy fear that he had felt a few minutes before had faded. The less he thought about what was happening to him, the better he felt. It was as though the something inside wanted him kept quiet. He raised his head as a thought struck him. More a sense, really: *Morgan is coming.*

"Hey, son," said the familiar gruff voice. "Thought I'd find you here."

Morgan, in that same stuffy suit, was leaning on his walking stick and chomping his stogie. "Oh. Hi," Rory stammered.

"Come along. No time to waste," the old man commanded and rapped his cane twice on the deck.

"Why?" Rory asked. "I mean, where?"

Morgan hobbled down the deck. Rory hesitated. The old man turned around and glowered. "What are you waiting for?" he demanded, and spat over the rail. "You've been dogging me since the moment we set foot aboard. If you want to learn what I'm about, you'll have to look sharp."

Rory nodded a couple of times, as if to convince himself to go along. He decided, despite all the strange occurrences, that Morgan was his friend. As with Lucy, it was rekindling feelings he liked and he didn't want to spoil it. He took a deep breath and they set off together.

"How did you know where I'd be?" Rory asked.

"Same way you knew where I was," Morgan replied.

Rory tried to make sense of his words as Morgan led the way up to Deck 3 and along the port side near the bow. He stopped at the bottom of a narrow ladder that rose fifteen feet up to a service platform behind the bridge. "Start climbing," he said.

Rory didn't like ladders. He looked up and shuddered. "I don't–" he began.

"Lay to it, lad! Watch your step. Don't look down. I'm right behind you."

With clenched teeth and fists wrapped tight on each rung, Rory went up. After what felt like a long climb, but was only twelve rungs, he crawled onto a small metal platform, with a railing on one edge and a door marked SYSTEMS CONTROL & SURVEILLANCE NETWORK at the back. He stood up and gripped the rail. He could see the whole ship, all the way to the stern and miles of ocean beyond. It was like a crow's nest and worth the climb. He tried not to think of having to go back down.

With a twist of the handle, Morgan pushed open the door and flicked on the light. It was a tiny windowless room. Behind a swivel chair, the wall was covered by panels and instruments, much like the control room Morgan had showed him the day before. He moved around as if he were home, checking gauges, tapping dials, switching on computer monitors, and jotting readings off indicators in his little notebook.

"Not much change. That's good." He puffed his dead cigar.

"What are we looking for?" Rory asked, nervous about being caught there.

"You may recall our talk of safety measures?" Morgan asked. Rory nodded. "Well, after checking ship systems for the past two days, I've found the trouble."

"Is that why you're here? Safety measures?"

"By my reckoning, the stabilizer controls are damaged," Morgan continued, ignoring the question.

"Stabilizer controls?" Rory was confused. *A ghost that does safety checks?*

"Let me show you." Morgan sat in the chair, with Rory looking over his shoulder. He flipped to a fresh page on his pad. He drew the top view of a ship, long and pointed at both ends, with propellers at the back. "This ship is powered by props deep in the water," he explained. "But standing so far above the sea can make her top-heavy." He added a couple of shark fins on either side of his drawing. "Along with ballast, these stabilizer fins extend from the sides to keep her from tipping."

Rory knew about stabilizers, but only in a general way. "The fins come out low on the hull, like a bilge keel, right?" he asked.

"Aye. Very good," Morgan replied. "They extend or retract depending on need. During a storm, they are essential to keep her from broaching to the wind."

"Broaching? Isn't that when a ship is stuck sideways, in a trough between waves?"

"Aye, and that makes it easier for the waves to swamp and capsize her. Very dangerous."

"It would take a monster storm to sink a ship this size," Rory remarked. "More than even a hurricane."

"True," Morgan replied. It bothered Rory that this was all he said.

"What's wrong with the stabilizers?"

"They may be indisposed to deploy."

Rory blanched. "They won't come out?"

"Aye."

"How do you know that?"

"I'm a naval engineer. It's my business to know."

Morgan Hewett's bio said he was an engineer, too. He wished Lucy could hear this. He had a rush of guilt, thinking that she was probably waiting for him on the foredeck.

Suddenly, the gist of what Morgan was saying came through like a flashlight on a dark night. "Are we expecting a storm?" he asked cautiously.

Morgan scratched his chin and let out a slow breath. "There's the question for the day, sure enough."

It wasn't Rory's question for the day, but it was a good one. *Maybe a ghost really knows what the weather will be.* "When?"

Morgan didn't answer. "As you saw last night, that file clerk posing as an officer threatened to lock me up if I go below again."

"Why do we need to go back down? Can't you tell the captain, or something?"

"Did it look to you like they were interested in heeding me?" the old man sneered. "No, we need to prove that the readings on the bridge don't match those below."

Rory didn't like the way this was shaping up. He had visions of the bulldog-faced officer beating him up this time. "He told me to stay out, too, you know."

"Aye. But you're young and resilient. You'd have no trouble staying clear of their sights."

Rory could only hope he was kidding. "I can't tamper with anything. I'd get caught."

"When the storm is up, they could think the fins are extended when they aren't. We'd go to the bottom." Morgan tapped the side of his head with a finger. "Think about that. You're a smart boy. We need another helping of last night's bravery, son."

"Bravery?" Rory didn't understand. "What for?"

"All you have to do is go below and get a reading off a dial that looks like that." He pointed at one of the gauges on the wall. It looked like every other gauge Rory had ever seen. "Don't quiver so! I'll tell you exactly what to do." He made a drawing of a control panel. "I gave you the gist of this yesterday, before that lummox interrupted us in the aft control room."

"Sure. I remember." Rory wasn't about to admit that he hadn't been paying attention.

Morgan explained where and how to take the reading as he made the drawing.

"I can't do that! I could make something go wrong," said Rory. But the thought of drowning was worse.

The old man fixed a fierce eye on him. "I thought you were a seaman! A seaman doesn't back down from duty when there's trouble. Now stop your blubbering and get a move on. The safety of all hands is at stake!"

There was no room for discussion.

To the Rescue

What am I doing? Rory finally reached the bottom of the ladder. Each rung had been agony and he was sure that climbing down was the bravest thing he'd done so far that week.

Unsure of what he was searching for, Rory headed back down below the waterline. It felt as if his feet were pulling him along. A thousand questions ran around his mind like race cars on a track and they sped by too quickly to glimpse any answers. *Is the old man really trying to save the ship? Why would a ghost want to save an ocean liner? Did he try and save the* Titanic, *too? Will there really be a storm?*

What he did know was that Morgan needed him. Morgan thought there was a storm coming and Rory believed him. Morgan was a mariner. They were both mariners. He'd said so, and that meant something special. *Maybe if I get this reading, he'll tell me what's going on. That is, if I have the guts to ask.* As it was, he wasn't sure he had the guts to go further.

His watch read 10:10. A quick stop at the foredeck proved that Lucy had probably come and gone. *Too bad. I really need her help.* Morgan said that he was brave, but Rory thought that Lucy was really the brave one. He felt stronger with her near.

He got off the main elevator at Deck 11 and crept down the stairs to Deck 15. This was getting very familiar. He poked his head out of the stairwell onto the engineering deck. Like the night before, it was brightly lit and loud and steamy, with big machines grinding away full-time. There was no day or night. The elaborate network of catwalks, stairs, and winding paths crisscrossed the whole space like a spider's web. Crouched under the stairs, he held his breath as someone passed by.

He imagined being James Bond trying to find a secret code. *In fact, that's close to what I've got to do,* he reminded himself. *Find a control panel, locate the hydraulics dial, and write down the reading off it.*

When the coast was clear, he scurried along the steel grate floor until he found the place where he and Lucy had rescued Morgan the night before. After that, his instructions said to turn to the port side and go up a short ramp. *Okay, so far so good. Next. Turn left and follow the rail for —*

He stopped. *Which side is port and which is starboard? There are no windows or signs. I should have been dropping breadcrumbs.*

Footsteps! He crawled through the rail and hid under the catwalk. Feet clanked by and faded away. He poked his head up. *All clear.* He sprinted on.

At the next junction, he squeezed behind a huge thumping metal box and wiped a sleeve across his steamy glasses to look over his crumpled instructions. "Panel is near the magneto room," he read. *This ship is almost 1,000 feet long! How am I supposed to spot a control panel on a wall as long as a skyscraper?* Suddenly, he didn't feel like a spy anymore. He felt like a scared little boy.

More men passed by. Things got worse. Every direction looked the same. He retreated along the catwalks, past rows and rows of pipes, machines, and panels, searching for anything familiar. Panic crept into his gut. It was spreading fast. *Where are the stairs? The elevator? Anything!* Shivering with dread and ducking out of sight at every sound, Rory feared that he'd never find a way out.

Then a strange thing happened. Almost as if a switch had been turned, he started to recognize the wall panels. He'd never seen them before, but they suddenly looked as familiar as the controls on his mom's car. Now he had two views of this deck. They both looked the same, but one he recognized and the other he didn't. He was both frightened and curious as he scanned the wall, looking for the stabilizer controls.

There they are. How obvious. "Now I can check that gauge." No one was watching. He pulled out his diagram and darted over. The big dial was the pressure. *Its reading should be —*

"What the hell are you doing there?"

"Augh!" Rory's knees buckled. The clarity of vision vanished and suddenly everything was strange again. He jammed the diagram in his pocket, like it was some incriminating evidence. For an instant, he wasn't sure even where he was.

"Well?" It was a man's voice.

He twisted around, half expecting to find a monster breathing down his neck. A wiry little man with fat fish lips, furry eyebrows, and a buzz cut stared accusingly at him. Cotton-mouthed, Rory squeaked out, "Nothing?"

"Then, what are you tampering with the equipment for?" the man demanded.

"Did you know there's a problem with the stabilizer readout?" Rory asked bleakly. He could hear his voice trembling.

"How would you know?"

"Isn't this the stabilizer control?"

The man looked past Rory's shoulder and eyed the equipment. "Yes, it is. What did you do?"

"I didn't touch anything. I just wanted to look."

"Well, you've had your look. Now we'll go to the security office and look at how much trouble you're in." He hooked Rory's arm in an iron grip and tugged. Rory resisted. Fishlips jerked and a pain shot up Rory's arm.

"*Oww.*" He didn't resist anymore and was marched smartly to the security office on Deck 10.

The security office was just a small room with a big desk and a couple of chairs. Pictures of sailing ships hung on white walls. Rory sat dejectedly, like a convict waiting for the warden. "This could be the last place I see before prison," he sighed.

He knew the real trouble would start once his mother found out. She would fuss and act surprised and then eventually get mad. Eddie would needle until she blew her stack and then they'd devise some nasty punishment that wouldn't end until he was a very old man. Even so, he had to admit that he got a real thrill from his adventure. He wished he hadn't screwed it up. *But I'm brave,* he told himself. *Morgan would be proud.*

The door opened. Rory braced himself. A balloon-shaped man stepped in and silently floated around the desk. He didn't sit. Instead, he hovered, clicking a pen that he held poised over a clipboard. He was soft and pink, with sausage fingers attached to puffy hands. But his beady eyes suggested that he wasn't soft on the inside. He clicked the pen again with a fat thumb.

"Mr. Dugan," he said, in a what-are-we-going-to-do-with-you tone. "I'm Mr. Biggins."

Rory nodded. And waited.

"And your stateroom is . . . ?" He clicked the pen again. "1140."

The pen made a note. "This is a serious matter. There are rules prohibiting these kinds of things. Do you know why we have rules . . . ?"

Rory was familiar with this kind of lecture. *Adults get this superior tone, making everything they say sound like a question when they talk to kids. But if you answer them, they get mad for being interrupted.*

"I'll tell you why we have rules. Safety. Can you imagine what kind of trouble we'd all be in if every passenger could go where they wanted and do anything?" Again the empty question. "No one would be safe, now, would they?" The pen clicked and Mr. Biggins was off on his speech, like a racehorse out of the gate.

While he talked, Rory wondered whether his mother had already been contacted and how long it would be until she arrived. He was sure they would get kicked off the boat in Greenland. *Are there any cities in Greenland? Would we have to live in an igloo?* While his mind wandered, he had another vision of being up on deck, looking out to sea. Like the two views of the stabilizer controls, the vision was very vivid. He felt like he was both here and there at once. Suddenly, it was gone.

Rory had the frightening thought that he might be going crazy. He focused on a big mole on the side of Mr. Biggins' nose that bobbed up and down as he talked. He watched until he heard the magic words that signaled it was time to tune back in: "Have you been listening?"

He nodded. "Yes, sir."

"I hope so, for your sake. I can't say what the captain will do when I make my report. There may be –" Mr. Biggins stopped short and looked up at the door.

There was a disturbance outside.

"Where is the boy?" bellowed a man's voice. "Don't spin me a yarn. I know he's here."

Rory gulped. *He sounds really mad!* He could hear a calm woman's voice in between the outbursts. If that was Eddie, he hoped the woman was his mom.

"You should really wait until Mr. Biggins is ready," the woman insisted.

"He's my grandson. Now let me through!"

The door burst open and Morgan limped in, towering over the surprised Mr. Biggins. A worried-looking young woman in a polka-dot dress followed on his heels. Rory jumped up.

"What is the meaning of this?" Mr. Biggins exclaimed.

"There you are," Morgan said. His voice was calm and even. "Biggins, is it? How do you do?" He stretched a hand across the desk. Mr. Biggins shook it and winced at the squeezing the old man gave his fat fingers. Morgan leaned on his stick and waved the woman from the room.

Rory was so relieved that it wasn't Eddie or his mom that he almost blew his cue. "Grandpa!" he finally said. He didn't know how Morgan had found him, but he sure hoped he could get him out of there.

"I understand that Rory has gotten himself in a mess," Morgan continued. "Aye. Boys will be boys, eh?" he chuckled.

"More than a mess, Mr. . . . ?" Biggins began in the same tone he had used with Rory.

"Hewett."

There it is. Morgan Hewett! Real proof. Rory stared dumbfounded at the old man.

"Fact is," Morgan explained calmly, "his mother was just married. New stepfather. Bit of a tyrant. Could spoil everyone's vacation, this could."

"I don't know . . . ," Biggins began. "If youngsters don't learn there are consequences. . . ." He clicked his pen.

"Of course. Of course!" Morgan tapped his cane twice. "Believe me, I was a naval officer – I understand these things. Man to man, I give you my word. I'll discipline the boy. Prefer to shield the family from disgrace. Keep it between the two of us. Know what I mean?"

There was a long pause. Rory tried his best to look repentant. Morgan kept his eyes intently on Biggins, who seemed to grow smaller, if that were possible.

"Well . . . he is only a boy, after all," Biggins conceded.

"You are a gentleman, sir, a gentleman," Morgan roared. The two men shook hands again.

Rory couldn't believe it. Morgan had pulled him out of the fire. After Mr. Biggins' ruffled feathers had been smoothed, Rory was ordered to apologize and told not to go below Deck 11 again. He promised he wouldn't and was released into his "grandfather's" custody.

They stood silently together, waiting for the elevator. Rory was in such a turmoil about this old man, he didn't know what to do next.

"Thank you," he said at last. "My mother would have –"

"Think nothing of it." Morgan put an arm around his shoulder. "It was a pleasure sidestepping that lackey. Besides, as you so nicely put it last night, we bluejackets should look after each other."

A Fiend's Curse

"How did you know where I was?" Rory asked. He was feeling almost giddy at having been rescued. The things he'd been up to would turn his mother ashen. Not to mention, he had surprised himself. He was like a different person.

"Same way you saw me," Morgan replied.

"*Huh?*" Rory said.

He helped the old man onto the elevator, pleased that Morgan took the arm he offered to lean on. He felt trusted. Rory knew there was something else going on – something dark and mysterious – and he had a lot of questions. But now he felt he could be more direct, less KFC, as Lucy put it.

Morgan brushed his whiskers with the back of his hand, pulled the chewed cigar stub from his pocket, and set it in the corner of his mouth. "Must be hungry after that adventure," he said. Rory couldn't argue with that.

The Danish he'd had for breakfast was long gone. Morgan tapped the button for Deck 7 with the gold cap on his cane. "We'll find something there."

Rory brushed his "whiskers," too. His heart raced as he readied himself to ask the big question about Morgan Hewett the ghost. *I'll wait until we've had some lunch,* he told himself as he thrust his hands in his pockets, emulating the old man's straight-backed stance. His fingers touched a crumpled paper. For a second he wondered what it was, and then remembered cramming Morgan's diagram in there after that fishlips guy caught him. He pulled it out and gave it to Morgan. "I guess I don't need this anymore." He blushed.

"What's this?" Morgan asked, plucking the paper from Rory's fingers. As he smoothed out the creases, his face drained of blood. He gulped. The change came over him so quickly that Rory thought he might be having a heart attack.

"Are you okay?" Rory asked.

Morgan's cheeks darkened, his eyes got hard as coal, and his jaw set like stone. He slammed a fist into the red STOP button so fast that Rory jumped. The elevator jerked to a halt and a buzzer started honking like a sick goose. Morgan shook the paper in Rory's face, then threw it on the floor. "You have been toying with me!"

"No, sir," Rory said. He snatched the paper up and saw he had pulled out the picture of Morgan and his wife he'd been saving for Lucy. He looked up apologetically. "*Um,* I can explain this," he mumbled. "You see –"

"Just who are you?" Morgan bellowed. "Out with it!"

"Stop yelling at me all the time!" Rory shouted. He couldn't take this roller-coaster ride. "I don't know what you want from me. I've done all the things you asked, but you're always getting mad at me."

"Who are you?" Morgan repeated.

"I thought I was your friend."

"You are, but –" Morgan stopped short. His expression changed from anger to fright. He drew back his lips in a twisted grin, like he was suddenly afraid of Rory. He had the look of the crewman in the aft control room.

Here we go again, Rory thought. "Are you Morgan Hewett? From the *Titanic?*"

"*Um* . . . yes?" He spoke softly, as though Rory might strike him.

"So this is *you* in this picture?" Rory said carefully.

Morgan swallowed. "Yes."

"So you are a ghost!"

Morgan sank to his knees and clutched Rory's sleeve. "Free me of this curse. I beg you!" he pleaded.

"What curse?"

"Vanderdecken's curse, my curse, the mariner's curse – call it what you will," Morgan sobbed. "So many deaths. Why must I be an instrument of it?"

"You mean on the *Titanic?*"

"Yes, yes. *Titanic, Andrea Doria, Yarmouth Castle, Afrique, Athena* . . . so many others. . . . Must I name them all?" His voice cracked with age. He tugged on Rory's sleeve. "Aren't they penance enough for my evil deed?" Rory found himself looking into the face of the most frightened creature he'd ever seen. "Have pity on me, I beg you."

Rory didn't know what to think. He wished that annoying buzzer would shut up. "What evil deed? Why are you cursed?" he said, as he pulled his arm free of Morgan's grasp and started slowly around the wall towards the button panel.

"That voice . . . ," Morgan muttered, as he let go of Rory's arm and slumped into the corner. "I listened to that voice."

"Voice?" Rory stopped himself, just as he was about to push the START button. *Voices. Visions. Dreams.* He no longer noticed the buzzer clanging away. "Whose voice was it?" he asked.

"I thought it was mine," Morgan whimpered, and ground his teeth bitterly. "As the *Titanic* tipped, I put Olivia in a lifeboat and the realization I was losing her forever swept over me. Then I heard a voice saying, 'Save yourself. Save yourself.'"

Rory remembered those were the same words Morgan had said to him in his dream two nights ago. A shiver shot down his spine as he realized the visions he'd been seeing were through Morgan's eyes! Visions of the past and the present. *That's how Morgan knew where I was. That's how I could understand the stabilizer panel. We were seeing through each other's eyes.* "Do you remember what happened?"

Morgan groaned. "Remember? *Hah!* I relive each tortuous second of that April night every waking hour, thinking, wishing it had happened differently. What if . . . ? What if . . . ?" He looked up at Rory, not really seeing him. The fear in his face had faded and was replaced by sorrow and regret. "What if she hadn't crashed into that iceberg? What if they'd had enough lifeboats? What if I hadn't . . . ?"

Without noticing, Rory had slid down onto his haunches, oblivious to the honking emergency horn. "What happened? On the *Titanic*, I mean," he asked.

"Once the bow dipped under, even the dullwits got the idea that the unsinkable ship was going down." His tone was dark and his eyes misty with memory, as though he were reciting a favorite story. "Panic struck like a hammer blow. Everyone stormed the boats. Some even jumped overboard to swim out. Idiots. They died as soon as they hit the freezing water.

"I was out of my mind with grief and panic and that voice – that incessant voice pounding in my head – drove me to what I did. I stumbled across one of the last boats being lowered. There was a scuffle at the far end. Panicked and angry men trying to board and only a midshipman to defend her with a pistol. Everyone's eyes were focused fore. In the confusion, I . . . I reached out of the dark and . . ." He cast his eyes down and let out his breath, as though telling this was the hardest thing he'd ever done. ". . . I plucked that boy right out of his seat! Stood him on deck. Took his place."

"You what?" Rory gasped. "You stole a boy's place? But . . . that's. . . ." There were no words. "Did he get on another boat?"

Morgan shook his head. "He was lost. Quiet as the grave, he stared at me as the boat was lowered. To this day I can't shut my eyes from his silent, accusing glare. I murdered him sure as I pitched him overboard myself. And I've been cursed by the devil ever since."

What? Rory thought his head would explode. *I killed a little boy, too. I hear that same accusing voice. I'm cursed, too!* He felt a shriek welling up from deep inside him. "*Save yourself!*" it taunted.

"Let me out! Let me out!" He hammered on the START button until the bell stopped ringing and the elevator started to move.

Behind him, Morgan wailed, "You have to release me from this curse! Do you hear me? I've paid for my sin!"

The doors opened. Two repairmen peered in on the makeshift confessional.

"You alright in there?" asked one.

Rory pushed past them and ran like the devil was after him.

Another Cursed Sailor

Head down, Rory skidded around corners and swerved into people. If he took stairs or tripped, he wasn't aware of it. He whipped past the gift shop, turned another corner, and cracked a crew door enough to slip through. *Click!* He was gone.

His one thought was to get to a safe place where no one could touch him. He ran down the corridor to the stairs, scraping his shoulders on the sides, and scrambled up a flight. Finally feeling far enough from danger, he slumped down in a corner, hugged his knees, and buried his face. There was no air. His chest was so tight he thought it might crush his heart. He gulped, but couldn't draw breath. Pins and needles pricked his face and hands like a thousand bee stings. He furiously rubbed and scratched, but it didn't help.

What a horrible story! How could anyone be so cruel? Drowning a boy! But he knew the real truth. *I'm cursed, too.*

I've been cursed since the day Ian died. This old demon or ghost or whatever he is has come to collect me! He'll throw me overboard and they can't do anything to him. He's already dead. A dead murderer.

Rory envisioned himself as that boy, as Ian, watching his only hope of life disappear over his head. These thoughts spun round and round like a whirlpool in a drain, and he was being sucked down with them. Lights flashed in his eyes. *I have to find Mom,* he thought. But he couldn't move. He just clutched himself tighter and started to rock back and forth, the world spinning.

"Breathe," said a soft voice. Warm hands rubbed his arms. "You're having an attack, or something. I'll get help."

It's Lucy! Her voice was like a lifeboat in a storm. He lifted his head. "Don't go." Rory clutched her arm. "I'm scared."

"Okay." She put an arm around his shoulder.

They sat quietly for some time, while Rory moaned and tried to keep from fainting. More than once she wanted to go for help, but each time he clung harder to her.

"Lucy?" he whispered at last, between short breaths.

"I'm here."

"He killed a kid." Simply saying it aloud was a relief. "He's a demon or possessed or something."

"Are you serious?"

"Serious as a coffin." In panted phrases, he told of how Morgan had groveled on his knees, sobbing out the story of his wicked deed on the *Titanic*.

"Wow! And he's afraid of you?"

"Worse," Rory replied.

"Worse?" Lucy asked in a hush. She relaxed her grip on him and stood up to face him. Rory noticed she was wearing the same bright red shorts she had on when they first met. "Tell me."

Rory hesitated. He didn't want anyone else to know that he was a murderer, too. He tried to collect his thoughts. He wanted to tell her, even needed to. His breathing had evened out and he felt a bit better. But he couldn't put his thoughts into words. After a bit he asked, "How did you find me?"

"You ran past me like a blur and I followed. Didn't you notice?"

He shook his head and sighed. "That was the scariest! I hope I never feel like that again in my whole life."

"I bet. I waited for you this morn, but you stood me up," Lucy said.

A twinge of guilt caught in Rory's throat. He had forgotten all about that. It seemed so long ago. "I'm sorry. I got there early and Morgan showed up. He sent me back down to the engineering deck and I got caught."

"No way."

Rory told her about the stabilizers and his trip to the security office.

"For a quiet kid, you sure know how to get into trouble. You're worse than me."

Rory chuckled. He was thinking that, too.

"I don't get it, Ror," Lucy said, and ran some fingers through her short hair while giving him her green-eyed work over. "If he's as scary as you say, why do you keep going back to hang with him?"

It wasn't exactly true that he chose to hang out with Morgan. He was almost compelled. He couldn't explain it. But that wasn't what was bothering him most. *Just tell her, stupid,* he said to himself.

"You have to promise not to spill this to anyone," he said.

She nodded and held a couple of fingers up in some sort of oath. "Honest."

He looked around to see if anyone was close by. "I killed a little boy once, too," he confessed. Hot tears rolled down his cheeks. Saying that out loud was so hard. He would almost rather have the old man throw him overboard than talk about this.

Lucy sat back down beside him and rubbed his back with the palm of her hand. "What happened?" she asked, her voice as gentle as a snowfall.

Rory forced himself to speak. "One day my little brother and I were at a friend's pool." He rocked back and forth, hardly believing the words were coming out. "A bunch of kids were playing in the yard. Ian threw his toy in the water." Each word brought him closer to reliving the event – the smell of chlorine, the sight of Ian struggling helplessly as the water swallowed him up. . . . He stopped. This was too hard.

"Tell me, Rory," Lucy said, her hand brushing his wet cheek. "Please."

His breathing was rapid, as though a monster was standing on his chest. "He jumped in to get it. He was scared and started thrashing around. I yelled for him to come out – 'You don't know how to swim!' I was going to go in after him, but it happened so fast. . . . I should have saved him!"

"Where was your mom?" Lucy's voice was barely audible.

"She came running, but when I reached out my hand, it was too late. I'd let him drown."

Lucy groaned. "Rory, I'm so sorry I pushed you in yesterday."

Rory sniffed. He was so numb just telling it that it was almost like he was listening to someone else. When he finished, his face and hands were soaked with tears. He felt completely drained. He had never before told the story to anyone, except when it first happened. He had stayed silent all these years, holding his poisonous shame and guilt inside.

"It wasn't your fault," she said, after what seemed like years of silence. "You were just a little kid yourself. You would have drowned, too, if you'd gone in after him."

He had heard those words a hundred times. From his parents, from counselors, from relatives, he'd heard them until he was sick of hearing them because he knew they were a lie. *How do they know I would have drowned if I'd gone in?* But somehow hearing them from Lucy made them sound different.

"You really think so?" he sniffed, and a load of guilt slid off his shoulders and into history.

"Of course," she insisted. "I wouldn't have done it, no matter how much I loved him. You didn't push him in, or anything. Your mom shouldn't have left you alone."

"You're not just saying that, are you?" They fell into a short silence.

Then Lucy said, "Maybe we better tell Grams and your parents."

"NO! Not about this," Rory shot back. "You swore to secrecy!"

"No, I mean about Morgan being a spook."

"Yeah, right." Rory was relieved. Then he tried to mimic Lucy's voice, "Say, Grams, Rory and me met this cursed ghoul on board who killed a kid on the *Titanic!* Way cool, huh?"

"Okay, okay. We don't have to put it like that," she laughed. "But, you have to agree that this is way over our heads, don't you?"

He nodded. They sat silently, listening to the hum of the engines.

"Let's tell," Lucy said.

"But who will believe us?" said Rory. He was too unsure of his mom's reaction and knew Eddie would make it worse. *That lets them out.* He didn't think the captain or purser would believe him. Especially after the stunts he and Morgan had pulled. *That leaves Grams.*

They took a roundabout route back to Lucy's stateroom, so they wouldn't run into Morgan. Grams was lounging on their deck in a lime green sundress, reading a book. She laid the book and reading glasses on a table and got up. "You look like you've seen a ghost."

"We have!" Lucy replied.

They both started talking at once, until Grams held up her hands to silence them. "Wait! Wait! Let's have some order here," she instructed. She led Rory to the deck and sat him down in the sun. "Rory first. Take your time. Lucy, fetch a drink for the lad. He looks pale as chalk. Are you hungry?"

Rory nodded. They never did get to lunch and that scare put a huge hole in the pit of his stomach.

"I can make you a sandwich," Lucy offered. "We have some stuff in the fridge."

Rory thanked her. He looked from one to the other and saw the worry on their faces. *I must look pretty bad,* he thought.

Grams sat down across from him and folded her hands in her lap. "Now. What happened?"

Rory looked past her to the glistening ocean and sky. His story seemed so unreal that he didn't know where to start.

"There's this old creep on the ship who —" Lucy began.

"Lucille! Let the boy talk for once."

"Sorry." She handed Rory a can of cream soda and went back inside.

He took a long swig and began. "Well, you see, it all started the other day when I ran into this old man. . . . I didn't mean to, but I wasn't looking and I knocked him right over." From there, his story poured out in bits and pieces. He wasn't sure if it made much sense. He left out the stuff about getting caught that morning at the stabilizer station and Morgan rescuing him at the security office.

"That's a very disturbing story," said Grams, when he finished.

Lucy slapped a fat sandwich down in front of him. "Sink your fangs into that." She then perched on the rail with a soda of her own.

He took a bite of the sandwich and froze with his mouth full. He looked up at Lucy.

She shrugged. "Potato salad."

"You made him a potato salad sandwich?" Grams asked in disbelief.

"It's good," Rory said, swallowing. *Anything would taste good, I'm so hungry.*

"Thanks." Lucy beamed. "That's all there was."

Grams sighed. "Have you told your parents?" she asked.

"My mom doesn't listen to me too much. She has a lot on her mind."

"On a cruise ship?"

"It's her honeymoon," Lucy explained.

"Oh. That's right," Grams replied. "Do you get along with your new stepfather? He seems a nice man."

Rory shook his head and took another bite of the sandwich.

"You believe us, don't you, Grams?" Lucy asked. She slid down and sat crosslegged on the floor, beside Rory's chair, and picked some potato chunks off his plate.

"I hardly know what to believe. But I see you are troubled by it and that's enough," she said.

"Why would he be on this ship?" Rory asked. Underneath it all, he was scared that Morgan was here to punish him for Ian's death. But he hadn't told Grams that part of the story.

"If – and it's a big if – your story is true, then no doubt he has a purpose here. God knows what it is," Grams agreed. "If he's making it all up, then your pictures are a coincidence. He could be playing games with you because he has nothing better to do. Or, he may really be crazy."

"Do you think he wants to hurt me?"

Grams considered for a moment. "He might. He sounds like a very troubled man. Especially all that stuff about demons and such."

"But if he is a ghost, or whatever, then he'd have bumped Rory off already, right?" Lucy added.

"Possibly. What worries me is that he thinks Rory may be a demon," Grams continued. "There are a couple of mental illnesses that make people behave like that. Some of them are dangerous."

"Do their pictures appear on the *Titanic?*" said Lucy.

"They do if they fake them," Grams replied. "Some obsessed people go to great lengths to be taken seriously."

Rory hadn't thought of that. Everything that had happened in the past couple of days was so real, and it could all be explained away, too. The more they talked about it, the more he thought it did sound like a fish story. He took another bite of the sandwich and sighed.

"Do you believe the *Titanic* story, Grams?" Lucy asked.

"I believe he told it to Rory," Grams agreed. "But, I don't believe it is true. In fact, the more I think about it, the more I think this whole adventure is cock-and-bull."

"You believe me, don't you?" Rory was suddenly in doubt. He hadn't told her anything about Ian.

"Yes, dear boy," she assured him. "I mean, it sounds like the old devil is making it up as he goes along."

"That's good. Right?" Rory asked. But deep inside, he felt that Morgan couldn't be dismissed as some crazy old loony. The pictures, his visions through Morgan's eyes, and the coincidence with Ian had to mean something.

"Why do you think he is so obsessed with the safety of the ship?" Lucy said.

"According to Rory, he thinks it's unstable," Grams said. "That might be the cause of his craziness right there."

"He's sure of that," Rory emphasized. "He mentioned a bunch of other ships he's been on, too. And some guy! A sailor named Vander . . . something."

"Vanderdecken! Thank you," Grams said. "I was just thinking of him, but I couldn't remember his name. He was the captain of *The Flying Dutchman*. Do you know that legend?"

"No," Rory replied. Lucy shook her head.

"I'm surprised with your thirst for ships that you wouldn't know this one," Grams said. She picked up a neglected iced tea that was melting on the table beside her and took a sip. "About three hundred years ago, there was a Dutch sea captain named Vanderdecken – Hendrick or Heinrich was his first name, I think – who set sail from Amsterdam to go all the way around the world in a ship called *The Flying Dutchman*. But by the time they reached the Cape of Good Hope, winter had set in."

"Which one is that?" asked Lucy. "Africa or South America?"

"Africa," said Rory. "Cape Horn is the other one."

"That's right," Grams agreed. "Vanderdecken decided to sail on, rather than wait until spring."

"That wasn't smart," Rory said. "Winter storms are the worst down there."

Grams nodded. "And that's just what happened. They met a terrible storm. The waves were so high that they dwarfed her masts and swamped the decks. The *Dutchman* was going to sink. But Vanderdecken was stubborn and refused to turn back, even though his crew begged him to.

"Instead, when things were at their most desperate, he made a deal with the devil. He said, 'I will do anything if you will see me through this storm!' The devil replied, 'I'll save your ship, but you shall be cursed to bring sailors misery for all eternity!'"

Rory leaned forward. "What was the curse?"

Grams raised a finger for him to be patient. "Well, *The Flying Dutchman* crashed into a reef. The crew were thrown overboard and drowned. But the captain had strapped himself to the helm and he drifted with the ship out to sea."

"That figures," Lucy said, leaning back on her hands. "Saved his own skin."

"So he was cursed to sail the seas forever, tied to the helm of the *Dutchman*, and any ship that sees her is doomed to sink," Grams concluded.

"Is that true?" Rory asked.

"Well, this is a story that is part true and part legend. But, like your old man's, it's hard to tell where the truth ends and the myth begins."

"Yeah, but I can't believe Morgan Hewett is 'forever cursed' to do safety checks. That's just so lame!" Lucy said.

Grams laughed. "Didn't you tell us that he said that this ship is going to sink?"

"He thinks we're headed for disaster," Rory corrected. "A storm, maybe."

Lucy said, "But there's got to be a reason for him to think the ship is in trouble."

"It might be entirely in his head," Grams concluded. "Whatever the reason, you'll have to tell your mother."

Rory looked doubtful. "I guess. But Eddie is a real jerk. He'll laugh at me."

"I know it's hard having a new parent." Grams put her hand on his arm. Her kind smile warmed him. "You think the world has ended when things change. You might even blame yourself. But, one day you'll discover that sometimes parents have problems of their own that have nothing to do with you. Not everything is your fault."

Rory wondered if his mom had told her about stuff. "What kind of problems could my mom have?"

"All people have problems," she replied. "Right now, we need to solve this one and that means telling her."

"Okay," he agreed.

"You get back to your stateroom. Let me ask around about Mr. Hewett. I'll talk to the purser, the captain, and maybe even the man himself. Then I'll come and visit with you and your family."

"Maybe you could tell the captain about the stabilizer readout. He could check to see if it's okay."

"Will do."

Having Grams help made Rory feel much better. He wasn't sure he wanted Mr. Biggins involved again, but he didn't say anything about that. He ate the last bite of the sandwich and got up to leave.

"Thank you for listening," he said, and started towards the door. Lucy jumped up and followed him.

"Lucille," Grams called. "Let Rory go. I want to talk with you."

"Okay," she replied and winked at Rory. "Meet me on the promenade as soon as you can," she whispered to him.

Rory nodded and left.

Both Lucy and Grams had lifted a huge weight off Rory's shoulders. *Maybe Morgan is just an old liar. Maybe I don't need to bury my feelings about Ian so deeply. Maybe life isn't so hard after all.*

Hearing *The Flying Dutchman* story had given Rory some clues to follow. Researching it might answer the question of why Morgan compared himself to Vanderdecken. *Maybe he's cursed to sink ships, not repair them,* Rory speculated. *It could explain why he is so obsessed with safety.*

Cautiously, to avoid running into Morgan, he made his way to Deck 8. Off the promenade was a little coffee shop called the Cyber Café that had computer terminals with Internet connections. There were twelve computers and two were vacant. He squeezed into a cubicle and typed in his cabin number. Then he typed Eddie's name in the billing dialogue box. He clicked OKAY and was in.

"Hi," Lucy said, behind him.

He was surprised she found him so quickly. "Did Grams give you any trouble?" he asked, without looking up.

"*Nah.* We're cool," she replied. "What are we looking for?"

Rory went to a search engine and did a web search on twentieth-century ship disasters. "We need more proof of who Morgan really is," he said.

"What if he's just crazy?" she asked.

"I'm not so sure."

"I saw him lurking around," Lucy said. "So I came another way."

Rory shuddered. He shot her a worried look. "Keep an eye peeled. Let me know if you see him."

"Roger that, Houston," she replied, and clicked her heels together.

The search came up with 110 web hits. "This could take some time to go through," he said, as he clicked the top one and started to read.

"That's what you said last night," Lucy joked. "I thought computers were supposed to make things faster, not slower."

"You still have to wade through all the info it gathers," Rory explained, as he started to download the next site. He was back on his own turf. Operating the computer was safe. And safe was what he needed to feel right then.

"What's that?" she asked, peering over his shoulder.

"That stuff about *The Flying Dutchman* gave me an idea. Morgan said he was on board a bunch of ships since the *Titanic*. He even named a few. I want to find out more about them."

"Why don't you just type in their names?" Lucy asked.

Rory grinned. "This might actually be faster." He clicked another subject heading. A dead end. "Or not."

Lucy pulled up a chair and eyed all the people nearby, staring at the blue screens. "Why do people on a cruise ship come here?" she asked. "Don't they get their computer fix at home?"

"E-mail is a big thing, Luce," said Rory. "You're way behind on that."

"What's wrong with the phone?"

"You'll understand when you get one. It's lots of fun. I bet you even get hooked. Instant messages, video streaming, the works."

"Not if I have to sit and –"

"Jackpot!" Rory exclaimed, and shook a fist in the air. "YES!"

He had found a web site that listed over sixty ship-wrecks. They sat in silence together, staring at the screen, while Rory quickly scanned down the list. Twenty were before the *Titanic*, eighteen were freighters or tankers, and the rest were passenger liners or ferries. Many had gone down from fires, some had collided with other ships, several had been swamped by bad weather, and a few had been torpedoed during World Wars I and II. The files had descriptions of the disasters, but none was as detailed as the *Titanic*'s. Somehow the story of the *Titanic* had become legend, while all the others were forgotten tragedies. Rory wondered if maybe Morgan was right in thinking that it was pride that made a legend of her.

Of all the names, four were of particular importance to him. "Morgan named these ships: *Andrea Doria*, *Yarmouth Castle*, *Afrique*, and *Athena*." He pointed at the screen. "It says here the *Yarmouth Castle* sank in the Caribbean after a fire in 1965, killing ninety-seven. The *Afrique* struck a reef after engine failure during a storm, on its way to West Africa in 1920. Only thirty-two passengers survived."

"That gives me the shivers, Ror," Lucy said. "Remember that we're on a ship, too."

"That's the point," Rory replied. "Here it says that the *Athena* was torpedoed by the Nazis in 1939, and the *Andrea Doria* sank after she was hit by another ship in 1956."

"So?"

"So. Morgan told me he was on all of those ships."

She still looked confused.

"Don't you get it? If he's cursed like *The Flying Dutchman*, then we're next!"

Rory Is Betrayed

ory and Lucy agreed to meet after supper, but Lucy seemed a bit strange. Almost as if she had some other plans, but didn't want to say what they were.

"I'll give you a call," she said, and left him scratching his head. He wondered if maybe she wasn't convinced yet herself.

No time to think about that right now. He didn't expect the same kind of response from his mother that he got from Grams. It wasn't that he didn't trust his mom, he just wasn't sure if she trusted him.

Claire and Eddie were in the stateroom getting ready to go out when Rory came in. They seemed pleased to see him, so he assumed that they hadn't heard from Mr. Biggins. Eddie was spread out on the sofa, buttoning up his butt ugly black-and-gold shirt. Mom was rinsing out something in the tiny bathroom sink. They asked him about his day and told him some of the things they had been doing. Everyone was in a good mood.

Rory sat on a corner of the bed. *It's now or never,* he thought, as he booted up his laptop. "Guys? Can I tell you something?"

Something in his tone caught his mom's attention. She came out of the bathroom and sat down beside him. "What is it, dear?"

"It's about Morgan, the old man that I've been hanging out with."

"Shoot," Eddie said, and leaned his big arms across the back of the couch.

Rory took a deep breath and waded in with as clear a story as he could tell. He described the events of the past three days, leaving out his feelings about Ian. Along with the pictures from his computer and a few questions for clarification, they seemed to take everything he said seriously. Eddie didn't even make any jokes. By the time he was done, Rory felt drained.

A silence followed, where Eddie and Claire exchanged looks. Rory waited tensely. Finally, it broke.

"I'd say the old guy was pulling your leg pretty hard there, sport," Eddie chuckled. "Did you and Lucy invent those web pages just for us? They're good."

His mom wasn't so amused. "I'm going to report him! He didn't hurt you, did he?" She sounded very worried. "He should be thrown off the boat."

"The photos are a nice touch, too," Eddie added. "You got a real talent there. Don't abuse it."

"This isn't funny, Eddie!" Claire said, and put her arms protectively around Rory. "That crazy old man might have hurt you."

Rory was floored. Neither reaction was what he expected. He figured he would have to do some convincing, but to be completely dismissed? "You don't get it. This ship is going to sink. See these other —"

"Rory, I know these past few years have been hard on you, but —"

There was a knock on the door. Eddie grunted and climbed to his feet to answer it. "Mrs. Donnelly. How nice to see you," he said, and stepped aside to let her in.

I'm saved, Rory thought. *Grams is here.*

"Hello, Abigail," said Claire.

"How do you do, all?" Grams replied, and came in. She was wearing the green sundress and a straw hat.

They exchanged a few pleasantries and offered her a soda before she sat down. Rory stayed on the bed beside his mom, while Eddy swept a space for Grams to sit on the couch. She started right in.

"Lucy brought Rory to me earlier this afternoon, white as a sheet and frightened out of his wits by something," she said, and cast her kindest smile at Rory. "He told me a story of an old man on this ship who sailed on the *Titanic* and carries a curse on his head."

"Yup, that's the one we heard, too." Eddie chuckled and handed her a plastic cup of cola, then leaned against the dresser and finished doing up his buttons.

"Honey," Claire asked Rory, "why didn't you come to me first?"

He looked guilty.

"Oh, I didn't mind helping out." Grams took a sip of her drink. "Very nice. Thanks much."

Claire exchanged a we'll-talk-about-this-later look with Rory.

"Anyway," Grams continued, "I didn't know what to believe, but I was convinced that the old man had at least said all those things. So, this past hour I did a bit of investigating to see if this Morgan Hewett is actually of any danger to your son."

Rory was relieved. He was sure she'd verify his story.

"I spoke with the purser, the first officer, and the cruise director. I couldn't find Mr. Hewett, and learned that there is more to this than I was told. It seems your son and Mr. Hewett have been quite busy together. At eleven o'clock this morning, for example, Rory was being questioned in the security office after tampering with the equipment on one of the restricted decks."

His mother's fingers gripped his arm and she blanched. "You what?"

Rory felt his cheeks get hot. He was afraid of that. "I didn't touch anything. I was just —"

"Save it," Eddie snapped.

Rory sank back and stared into the space straight in front of him. *I'm cooked. Stick a fork in me.*

"Please go on, Mrs. Donnelly," Eddie said.

"Well, Mr. Hewett claimed to be Rory's grandfather. Rory even called him Grandpa."

"What?" Claire exclaimed again.

"The two of them put on quite an act together," Grams said. "'Grandpa' claimed that Rory's stepfather was nasty and asked that the boy be released into his custody. Which he was."

"What?" Claire said, a third time. "I don't believe it. I mean, I believe what you are telling me. I'm simply shocked."

"I'm sorry to have to tell you this." Grams looked at Rory with stern compassion.

Rory didn't dare look up. He could feel two pairs of angry eyes boring holes in his head. The mother of all punishments would come down on him after this.

"Unfortunately, that isn't all," she continued. "According to a security report from last night, they stopped Mr. Hewett from tampering with the same equipment. Then Rory appeared and claimed that he was the old man's grandson. Rory swore to the officer in charge that 'Grandpa' was crazy and needed his medication. Mr. Hewett then exhibited signs of disorientation. They said if it wasn't true, it was well rehearsed. They took him at his word and released both of them."

"You've got a lot of explaining to do," Eddie said, through his teeth.

"I've never in all my life heard such a story!" Claire exclaimed, practically shaking him. "Rory, is this true?" She used a quiet tone that Rory knew was the calm before the storm.

Rory didn't look up. He nodded almost imperceptibly. Somehow, what he had done didn't seem as bad as it sounded. But it sure sounded bad now. He was about to say something, when his mom told him to shut up.

"All of this is bad enough, but to involve Mrs. Donnelly. You should be ashamed of yourself." She was exasperated. "Is there anything else, Abigail?" she asked.

"Not about Rory's adventures," Grams went on, giving him a sidelong look. "But, from what the security officer said about Mr. Hewett, it holds with what Rory has told us. The man has been obsessive about the safety of the ship and has been pestering the crew nonstop since we set sail. Some of the problems that he has told them about have turned out to be true." She turned to Rory. "You'll be pleased to hear that the condition of the stabilizers is being investigated. The purser could give me no information on Mr. Hewett, but he plans to question him this evening."

"Lucy can tell you that I didn't make this stuff up!" Rory blurted. "She was down there with me last night. She knows they were going to beat him up! She knows. Just ask her!"

Grams cleared her throat. "Lucy swears she was at the disco last night."

What a lying little sneak! She bailed on me. There was nothing left to say. He dropped his head.

After an awkward pause, Grams got up. "I should leave you to work this out."

Embarrassed, Claire said, "Thank you very much for bringing this to us. I'm really sorry that Rory dragged you into his fantasy. I don't know what is going on here, but we'll sort things out. Rory, you owe Mrs. Donnelly an apology."

Rory couldn't figure how things got so turned around. "I'm sorry, Mrs. Donnelly," he muttered.

At the door, Grams said, "I don't know what the truth is, Rory, but you best stay away from that old man. He may really be dangerous, whatever his story is." She said good-bye and left.

Rory had never felt so stupid in his life. His mom and Eddie jumped all over him, like dogs on a steak. They yelled, cursed, and scolded. They were so angry that it made Rory cringe. Finally, the squall passed and they grounded him. Said that if he left the cabin for the rest of the day, he'd really know what trouble was.

"We'll deal with this when we get back home next week" was all his mom would say on the subject of his punishment. She said it in such a quiet voice that it was unnerving. Then she told Eddie to keep his trap shut and they went out.

As soon as they were gone, Rory flew into a rage all his own.

"Leave me alone!" he screamed at the door. "I don't care if you don't believe me!" He felt humiliated, offended, helpless, and confused all at once. He kicked the dresser and swept everything off it onto the floor.

"What do you know, anyway?" he continued, fueling his anger. "There really is a demon and you don't care. Well, watch out when he comes looking for you!"

What bothered him most, though, was Lucy. "You betrayed me! I trusted you and told you secrets and everything!" He had bared his soul to her – told her more than he'd ever told anyone. His gut ached at the thought of her laughing at him. Like everyone else, she probably decided he was just a geek.

"I hate you, Lucy Pritchard!" he yelled. *Now Grams and Mom think I'm a lying idiot.*

Splat! He threw a stale jelly donut at the wall. The sound was satisfying.

"I hate you, too, Fat Eddie – you poundcake! You're a stinking, meddling, puss wad! So there."

Splat! He threw another donut. It felt good.

"And you, too, Morgan Hewett! You said you were my friend. Well, I don't need you!"

He had run out of donuts. He threw the plate. *Crash!*

"I know better than to trust anyone. Serves me right. Well, so what if you don't believe me? I'll show you. I'll prove it."

He started to throw things around and scream like a madman. First the pillows, then the books, a chair, anything he could lay his hands on, he threw down and stomped on while he cursed and yelled. He'd never been this angry or violent before in his life and it scared him. He was like a person possessed. He aimed his laptop – his precious computer – at the mirror and saw his face drawn and contorted, his eyes wide, his cheeks bright red with rage. A sudden chill, like a blast from an air conditioner, hit him and stopped him dead. He recalled all the other times he'd felt that cold fear in the past few days as painfully as if he were being sliced open by a knife. Something was inside him. Something that fed off his rage and fear.

With shaky hands, he put down the computer and ran to the bathroom to splash water on his face. One look in the bathroom mirror and he could see that things were already better. Especially his eyes. For an instant during his rage, his eyes had become the hunted eyes of Morgan in the elevator!

Rory paced for a few minutes until he was calmer. The cold had gone, the nightmare passed. Now he believed more than ever that Morgan was a ghost of some sort and that he, himself, was connected to it. If he didn't find out what Morgan was up to, there would be serious trouble. Both for him and for the whole ship.

Ignoring the mess he'd made, including jelly donuts dripping off the wall, he settled down with his computer. "Morgan is cursed by a demon to travel from doomed ship to doomed ship. That's why he's running around, looking for problems," he said. It helped to talk out loud. The strange feelings that led him below last night, the visions, and now the cold fears, added to the pictures on the Internet and Morgan's own story, all pointed towards the same horrible conclusion. "He knows the *Sea Lion* is doomed."

That chilled him to the bone. *I have to think! Why won't anyone believe me?* His worst nightmare was about to repeat itself. Everyone he loved would drown and he wouldn't be able to save them. And he would drown, too.

He was relieved that Grams had alerted the purser about the stabilizers. *That might be the answer.* "Use your head, Rory," he said. "If all of the ships that Morgan was on meet disaster, there are no exceptions. So if the stabilizers get fixed, that isn't the real problem. Something else will happen." *But what? And when?*

"I've got to convince someone that this is all true." Lucy had sold him out, which explained her weird behavior when she left him. He logged on to his E-mail and sent a message to the webmaster of the *Titanic* Internet page. He would tell him if Morgan Hewett was real.

All he could think about was to wish that Morgan weren't on the ship. Then she wouldn't be doomed. "So, how do you get a cursed whatever-he-is off the ship in the middle of the ocean?" A terrible voice deep in the back of his mind said, *It doesn't matter how, as long as you do.* Rory felt ashamed for even thinking that. It reminded him of the bad thoughts he'd had about Ian.

When Claire and Eddie returned, they stood speechless in the doorway, staring at the disaster Rory had made of the room. Claire told Eddie to stay out of the way and she helped Rory pick everything up, even wipe the jelly off the wall. Then they all went to supper. She was unusually calm and quiet the whole time. Even Eddie was subdued.

The dining room was twittering with the usual conversation. Rory didn't say anything except to answer questions. He didn't see Lucy and told himself he didn't care. He was very hungry and ate roast beef, all the trimmings, and two desserts. He was on his best behavior. Nothing was said about his adventures or punishment. There was an uneasiness in the air between his mother and Eddie that Rory hadn't noticed before. He wished he was home and this was all over.

The three of them went back to the cabin together, and Rory curled up on his bed with his computer and a couple of comic books. Eddie changed and said he was going to the casino. Claire decided to stay in for the evening. After Eddie went out, she sat down beside Rory while he checked his E-mail.

"What did you do this afternoon?" she asked quietly. "I mean, besides trash the place."

"Nothing," he shrugged. He kept tapping computer keys.

"You must know that you can't go around getting into trouble and lying to everyone about who you are."

Rory didn't answer. Two messages were downloading. One from webmaster@titanic.uk and the other from his dad. He clicked on the first one excitedly.

Claire was saying, "I'm sorry if you think we're being unfair —"

"Mom!" Rory interrupted. "Listen to this. It's a message from the *Titanic* webmaster. 'Dear Mr. Dugan, I did a quick search of my records and find that there was a survivor named Morgan Hewett (passenger #245). My site has a short bio on him and a picture. If you have further information about him, I would be pleased to add it to our collection. Sincerely, Tom Reynolds.'" He looked up at his mother, his eyes glowing with pleasure. "So there," he added.

Claire smiled and asked to see the message. After reading it herself, she turned the computer back to Rory.

"All that proves is that this old man is pretending to be Mr. Hewett."

"With the same face and photo?" Rory asked. He was surprised at her stubbornness.

"Don't take that tone with me, young man," she said defensively. "You're still in a world of trouble."

"You don't even believe him?" Rory pointed at his computer. "What will it take? Does the ship have to sink?"

"Would you believe it, if I told that story to you?"

"I would if I trusted you."

"I see. You think it's a matter of trust," she replied, with a sigh. "If it's trust, then why did you lie to the crewmen and sneak around the ship like that?"

Rory squeezed his lips tight in frustration. "Don't you believe anything I said about Morgan?"

"You know what we learned about him?" Claire asked.

Rory didn't think it could be worse than what he knew.

"He's a crazy old man who's been meddling where he doesn't belong. After hearing our complaint, and it wasn't the first, the purser said they may put him off the boat in Halifax." She sounded exasperated. "Honestly, I don't know how you got mixed up with him."

Rory remained silent.

"I simply can't get through to you anymore, Rory. I know our family has had its share of grief. But we have to move past it. This isn't about Ian, is it?" she asked cautiously. "I mean, you must admit that a story about an old man who drowned a little boy has a very familiar ring. Our little boy wasn't drowned by an old man or by you."

"I'm insulted by the innundo," he said flatly.

"The what?" she laughed.

"Innundo? You know, implication?"

She smiled. "Innuendo." Her tone softened and she wrapped her arms around his head and squeezed him affectionately. "I mean no innundo. You're so withdrawn sometimes. I don't know where the truth ends and your fantasies begin."

The light went on. "You think I made the whole story up, don't you?"

"We've heard a lot of tall tales from you these past couple of years," she sighed. "Too many to even remember. You're failing at school and you've dropped all your friends. All you do is read and daydream. What should I believe?"

Rory was silent.

"We all miss him," she continued. "If I could trade places with him, I would." Her voice was ragged, and when Rory looked up he saw she was crying. Strangely he wasn't moved. "I lost both of you that morning and I so desperately want you back." She leaned her head on his shoulder. "You have to join the living again sometime, Rory. You're too hard on yourself."

"You trusted me and look what happened," he mumbled.

"Is that what this is about?" she asked. "I made a mistake, not you. It wasn't your fault. Whether you were a small boy or an experienced old sailor, it wasn't your fault. I have to bear the guilt of Ian's death."

Really? Does she really think it's her fault? Rory tried to wrap his mind around that, but he couldn't. He had borne the weight of Ian's death for so long that he couldn't accept this. At least, not now.

"What if . . . I mean, then, what if this stuff is true?" he stated matter-of-factly, changing the subject. "What if this ship is going to sink?"

"Don't talk like that, Rory. It scares me," Claire said, her hand reaching protectively for her throat. "This ship is very safe and just because there is a crazy old man who thinks it's going to sink doesn't mean it will."

"Don't you think we should make sure?"

"Can't you let go for even a second? We all suffered when we lost Ian. It broke our family up. But it doesn't have to be that way forever. I know it feels like I've been far away, but think about how far away you are all the time. You don't let anyone in. Can't we meet somewhere in the middle?"

Rory's lips tightened. He had never thought of it that way. He so desperately wanted things to be the way they were before. But he was beginning to realize that that would never happen. He tried to let people in, but they kept hurting him. Lucy and Morgan were the latest examples of that. *It's a mistake to trust anyone. They let you down every time.*

The phone rang and Claire reached over to pick it up. "Hello?" she said. She smiled at Rory and extended the phone to him. "It's Lucy."

Rory shook his head and crossed his arms. "I don't want to talk to her."

"She's your friend, Rory," Claire said, with a hand cupped over the receiver.

"Not anymore."

"This is what I am talking about. You have to trust people."

"Not when they betray you."

Claire shot him a stony glare and then returned to the phone. "I'm sorry, Lucy, but Rory is being stubborn and won't come to the phone. Maybe you could try again later. Yes, we'll be up. Okay. Bye." She hung up. "That was rude."

"She went down there with me last night. She lied to save her own butt."

"The fact is, you both lied. Does that make either one of you better than the other?"

Rory couldn't answer that one.

14

The Trick of the Curse

Rory had a terrible dream. Hands covered in grease, he was down below tearing apart the stabilizer controls. He took a wild pleasure in this work, imagining that he was saving the ship, but knowing in his heart that he was destroying it. He could hear himself cackle with pleasure. The dream was so vivid that he could feel the gritty sweat on his face and arms.

His leg jerked like he was kicking something and it woke him up. He sat up panting. It was pitch-black. His hands were clammy and his face was covered in cold sweat. When he closed his eyes, he could see his greasy hands still at work unhooking the hoses and gauges with a wrench. He felt an urgent need to find Morgan. He didn't know why.

You have to kill him to save the ship, said an evil voice deep inside him. *Where did that come from?* he wondered in a sudden panic.

He slapped his glasses on and scanned the room. The glowing dial of his watch read 3:30. Both his mom and Eddie were asleep. The seas were a bit rough, but all else was quiet. With sudden urgency, he crept out of bed and poked around in the dark until he found his clothes. Quietly dressing, he paused every few seconds to make sure that the breathing in the next bed stayed slow and even. One step at a time, he crept to the door, slid the chain off, and slipped through.

Squinting in the bright light outside his room, he ran down the hallway not quite knowing where he was going. It felt as though his legs were carrying him along without his say-so. He headed straight for the crew stairs and, with a great effort, diverted himself to the elevator. But something was pulling him toward those stairs. Forcing himself into the elevator car, he pushed the button for Deck 8. As the elevator shot up, he started getting chest pains and found it hard to breathe. The vision of a cabinet full of plumbing pipes swam before his eyes and the door in front of him got blurry. *I can't breathe! I have to get out of here.*

As soon as the doors were open, Rory headed for the glass doors to the deck. There was no one around. He thought that fresh air was all he needed. But each step forward was like walking with cement blocks tied to his shoes. He stopped to catch his breath, totally confused. His body wanted to turn around and it took great will to stay where he was. "Is this a dream? I should be in control of where my body goes!" he said defiantly. But the more he refused to do his body's bidding, the more painful it felt. And the pain was scaring him.

The ship lurched and nearly knocked him down. *Maybe I can relax for just a second,* he thought. But as soon as he did, his legs started running. They carried him to the main stairs and it felt so good that he didn't resist. His vision cleared and breathing became easier.

Down the steps, two at a time, he raced. His possessed legs took him right past his own cabin on Deck 11 and down the crew stairs. He got to the engine deck and realized with dread where he was going. Fear swallowed him up as though he'd plunged into the deep end of a pool. He jerked to a stop at the door.

"NO!" he yelled. "I tell my body what to do." He stood in the steamy hot hall, staring at the web of catwalks that he now knew well, swaying back and forth, struggling for control. Slowly he turned around, an itch burning under his skin. *I have to do something. But what?*

Kill him, whispered the dark voice.

"Shut up," Rory told it.

The ship rocked and he lost his concentration. In a flash, his feet were clamoring down the catwalks, straight towards the stabilizers. He couldn't fight it and he did some of the running himself. *If you can't beat 'em, join 'em,* he thought stupidly. The bad weather was making the ship roll so much that he grasped the railings on both sides of the narrow grate as he ran. Finally, he reached the end. Panting and clutching his sides with pain, he looked up to see Morgan, bent over the stabilizers. He felt the sweat go cold on his skin and he could see his breath. *I am in the presence of evil.* He knew now that this was what the cold was and the foul smell of bad meat that accompanied it.

Here was the demon that Morgan had been so terrified of. It was Morgan himself! Rory was under its spell, too. He could see now that it had been happening to him all week, a bit at a time, and now he was totally helpless.

"It's about time you got here," said the demon, with a cackling laugh.

Rory caught his breath as the old man turned to look at him. He had become so decomposed and withered that his skin looked like it had been glued onto his skeleton. A nasty, sinister snarl twisted his face, and his whiskers looked like coconut hairs, poking out at the sides. His evil eyes blazed behind the tiny glasses.

"What do you want with me?" Rory cried.

"Can't have you fouling up the works anymore."

To his horror he watched as the demon, with sleeves rolled up and bony hands covered in grease, tinkered inside the open panel. It hadn't been a dream. He had been seeing through the demon's eyes. The pipes were exactly the same. Instinctively he knew if there was any chance of survival, he must show courage, no matter how hard it was.

"Are you going to sink us?" Rory demanded.

"Course not. I'm trying to save her," the fiend replied, curling his lip up in a smirk. He pointed with his chin. "Hand me that wrench. This hydraulic coupling is giving me grief." He laughed. The guts of the stabilizer controls, like those in Rory's dream, were now in pieces on the floor.

Rory clenched his hands by his sides, refusing to budge. *I must resist,* he kept repeating to himself. But it was like trying not to scratch a bad itch. "How many ships have you sunk? All the ones you mentioned were destroyed," he said, with great effort.

"Hand me the wrench, boy!" the fiend snapped.

Rory jumped. His arm reached for the wrench and he fought to stop it. His whole arm shook, as though he were waving good-bye. With an oath, the demon pulled one hand free and grabbed the tool himself. Rory's arm was released and he fell back exhausted.

"I don't sink ships. They're already doomed. All I can do is find the problem. Maybe warn the crew, reduce the damage." It sounded more like Morgan's voice this time. He stopped working and pointed at the pipes. "You don't think I caused this mess, do you? No. I'm only along for the ride."

"You just *think* you're fixing it," Rory replied, "but you know deep down that's not true."

"Poppycock!"

"How many ships?" Rory repeated, sweat breaking out on his hands and face despite the chill.

Morgan yanked at a tight bolt. "Fifteen. Not all went down thanks to me."

Rory stuck out his chin defiantly and curled his fists so tight that it made his fingers hurt. "You have to stop right now!" he commanded.

"Sounds like you're growing some whiskers," Morgan said irately. "Too bad you haven't brains to go with them."

The deck shook and pitched Rory into the rail. Some tools slid down the catwalk. He could feel the increased intensity of the storm outside with each smack the ship took. It would take all the courage and strength he could find, invent, or scrape together to stay alert.

"While you are still in control of yourself, you have to get off the ship. That's the only way to save it," Rory persisted, trying desperately to stuff his fear back down. "I know how hard that is. But the demon inside you is what causes the disaster."

Morgan reached up and leaned over the controls to flick a switch. The dials stayed the same. "Damnation!" he swore. He turned to Rory and snarled, "You're befuddled, boy. If we don't repair this, we'll go to the bottom. Now pick up those tools and look sharp!"

To his surprise, Rory didn't flinch. "No! The storm will sink us. Not this."

"You insubordinate pup! I'll have you lashed to the mast for this." *It's still good old Morgan!*

"The purser told Grams he'd check the stabilizers. Why wouldn't they fix them if they know they're broken?" Rory said.

"Why'd the skipper of the *Herald of Free Enterprise* leave the ferry doors open, killing some 190? Why'd the crew of the *Morro Castle* ignore safety measures, costing 137 lives even though passengers complained loudly and often?" Morgan retorted.

"Were you on those ships?"

"Aye."

"How did you escape?"

"Ran for the lifeboats like everyone else, I suppose."

"You see?" Rory cried triumphantly. "You keep replaying what happened the first time."

"*Bah!*" Morgan threw down his tools in frustration. "These hoses are so old, it's no wonder there's no pressure. They nearly crumble to the touch."

Rory could feel the old man's intense rage and impatience come off him like heat. *I have to get through to him, no matter what.*

You'll have to kill him! It's the only way, said the voice, more insistently this time. *Save yourself.*

"No, I won't," Rory told it defiantly.

You hesitated and Ian died. Don't make the same mistake again, said the voice.

That hurt. Rory's heart thumped while he looked straight at Morgan. "How did you know yesterday that there would be a storm today?" he asked.

The old man broke his gaze away from the panel and turned his devil's eyes on Rory. "Reason," he sneered and flicked his forehead. "Once I discovered faulty stabilizer hydraulics, it was clear the only way to make them dangerous was foul weather."

"That's backwards!" Rory argued. "If it weren't for the curse, the stuck stabilizers wouldn't matter. It's the storm that's the problem!"

"Just because I reasoned a storm would come doesn't mean that I willed it," Morgan countered.

"A storm big enough to sink this ship would show on all the satellite maps. The captain wouldn't steer us there." *That's reason,* Rory thought, or so he hoped.

But Morgan wasn't listening to reason. "This is the way it must be done," he insisted, with finality.

Rory snapped. "You're a coward!" he yelled. "You didn't leave the *Titanic* for your wife. You were just scared to die." He felt his own anger burning, rising, and feeding on the fear.

Good boy. Turn it to hate, said the dark voice.

"Only a fool isn't afraid to die," Morgan spat back.

"But you're already dead! You've been dead for over ninety years."

Suddenly the air was cold again.

"I've taken as much from you as I intend to, you whelp!" spat the demon. "Hewett gave his soul to me the minute he snatched that boy." He moved menacingly towards Rory. "And now it is your turn."

Rory didn't know how the wrench got into his hands as it swung loosely at his side. *All I have to do is clobber him with it and the whole thing will be over,* he told himself. *What's so bad about that? It will save the ship.*

Do it! goaded the voice inside. *DO IT! You let poor Ian die to save your sorry skin. Do it again. Strike him down.*

Rory backed up and raised the weapon as the old man stepped closer. The cold stench of rotting meat got stronger as he approached. It clogged Rory's nose and throat so that he didn't even want to breathe. The old man was weak. All he had to do was swing the wrench and it would all be over. *Save yourself. Save yourself.* It was almost overpowering.

He closed his eyes and heard the wrench clatter to the floor. "I can't!" he wailed. "I didn't kill Ian. That wasn't my fault."

"Then die!" the demon screeched.

Rory felt cold fingers grip his throat. They were like writhing worms, squishy but hard underneath, as they bit into his neck like bony bird talons. Rory tried to twist free, but the demon slammed him against the rail. He knew it would do no good to fight. *If he wants me dead, I'm dead.*

"You've no right to call me a coward. None at all," the being whined. "I trusted you. We were shipmates." It was the demon's voice, but Morgan's words. For an instant Rory thought he saw the old man trying to peer out through the demon's mask he was wearing. He knew the struggle that was raging behind it between Morgan and the demon. He'd been struggling himself ever since he'd woken up from that nightmare.

"Help me," the old man moaned.

"You have to break the curse," Rory choked out. "You should have died in this part of the ocean a long time ago."

The cold fingers around Rory's throat had released their pressure, but he could feel them shaking with the effort.

"I'm not here by choice," Morgan wailed. "Do my best. But it wearies what's left of my soul, it does. Could let the cards fall, I could. You'd all go to the bottom. No difference to me, either way. As you say, I'm already dead."

Rory gulped. His head started spinning as the demon emerged again and filled his mind with cruel visions. His skin began to buzz with the sensation of bugs crawling on him – bugs he couldn't brush off. Images of ships on fire, people tumbling overboard, torpedoes exploding and carving huge holes in hulls swam before his eyes. He saw people screaming and fleeing from water that climbed over the rail to snatch their lives. It was overwhelming. Scenes of sinking ships and wretched survivors kept coming. He saw men in lifeboats, pulling bodies out of the water; ballrooms tipped on their side, with furniture and human forms floating in the debris. A fear so deep boiled up, acrid and coal black. At last, a silent scream reached his lips as the pain and fear of everyone that had been lost became his own.

"Now you see it!" shrieked the demon. "Yes, there lies your fate, too."

Rory's lungs were on fire for lack of air. He could feel himself tumbling and spinning into the deep black well of empty, certain death. Once there, he would become a servant of this fiend, just like Morgan. "But I've done nothing evil," he heard himself gasp. "It wasn't my fault."

Through the roar in his ears, Rory could hear an outcry down the walkway and feet clattering towards them. The demon's grip on him loosened. The spell was broken. He slumped to the floor and felt the sweet trickle of air fill his lungs.

"There is time for you yet!" the demon cursed and hobbled off faster than Rory would have imagined. Without resisting, he felt his body slip through the rail and roll under the catwalk to hide as three men ran up and stood over him.

"Hey, you!" called a deep voice after the old man.

"It's that foul old geezer," said a second man, whose voice sounded familiar. "Charlie, get after him."

"Gotcha," Charlie replied, and ran off.

"Look at this, Sam," said the third. "He was buggering up the stabilizer hydraulics."

"Damn," said the familiar voice. "Call the bridge. I'll check the damage."

As the ship lurched and threw them all off balance, one of them started to work on the system and the other reached for the phone.

Rory let out a breath. He sensed the demon's spell was broken for the moment. He was in control. He could move his hands and legs without any strain of being pulled like a doll. From his hiding spot, he listened as the two men looked over the mess that Morgan had left. As they talked and argued and clanged tools, he realized they might be there for a while.

He tried to think of pleasant things so that he wouldn't panic. He remembered the E-mail he got from his dad. Dad's response had been much like Mom's: "Don't let your imagination carry you away, son." *Not much comfort at all. What would he say if he could see me here?*

Much as he wanted to, he couldn't stay still forever. Something sharp was poking into his back and dug into him with every jolt of the ship. On top of that, he recognized the familiar voice. It was the guy with the fish lips, who'd caught him there the previous day.

The men were right over top of him. If they looked down they'd see him under the floor, as though they were just on the other side of a sheet of ice. *This is like being in a war movie,* he thought, *where soldiers have to hide from the enemy for hours in the mud, using a straw to breathe through.* He hoped that the men could fix the hydraulics and then everyone would be safe. *Maybe the demon's plans are foiled this time. Maybe I've delayed things enough to save us. . . .* Much as he hoped for it, he didn't believe it.

Finally, the work stopped. Rory held his breath. Almost being killed by a demon was bad enough, but this was agony.

"I'll go check on the relays. You try and get pressure from here."

"I'm on it," Fishlips replied.

While Fishlips worked right over his head, time was running out. His vision went cloudy and he suddenly found himself out in the storm. This time it wasn't just a visual scene. He could hear and feel the wind and pelting rain whipping around his head. They were on the lifeboat deck and Morgan was struggling with someone – he was trying to throw the demon overboard. Rory felt the intensity of the battle as Morgan tried to take command of his own body long enough to get over the railing and destroy the demon. But Rory knew that Morgan was as terrified of water as he was. Then the vision disappeared. Rory was back looking up at the feet of the workman through the catwalk.

I have to make a break for it. Morgan needs my help. I'll roll out when Fishlips has his back to me, and then bolt down the ramp as fast as I can. It's the only way. His heartbeat pounded in his head. He knew if he was caught, he'd never get another chance. *Here goes nothing. Three . . . two . . . one. . . .*

"Hi, there," said a girl's voice.

Rory jammed on the brakes! He raised his eyes.

"Maybe you can help me out? I'm looking for a friend of mine."

It was Lucy.

The Demon's Fury

"What are you doing here?" Fishlips demanded, standing right over Rory's head.

"It's okay. My friend said I could meet him here," Lucy replied coyly.

"This isn't a playground. There is a storm outside!" Fishlips growled. "Get aloft!"

Rory couldn't imagine what she was doing there, but he had never been so glad in all his life to hear someone's voice. He put all his muddled energy into thinking of a way to get her attention. *If I can move my hand a little bit, I might be able to poke her foot through the grating. But Fishlips might notice, too.*

"A guy named Paul?" Lucy persisted, while gripping the railings with both hands. "Tall dude with a beard? He said he'd give me a tour. He was at the captain's table for dinner on – I think it was Tuesday. I'm not sure."

Rory noticed her looking around. *She's looking for me!*

"I don't know any Paul. Did he tell you to come here in the middle of the night? In the middle of a storm?" Fishlips was suspicious.

"Yeah," Lucy replied. "He wore one of those white uniforms like they wear upstairs."

Rory slowly twisted his arm so that it was free. He moved very carefully. Sudden motions would get them both looking down. Just then he was hit with a spasm. His legs tensed up and tried to roll him out.

"An officer?" Fishlips said. "And he said you should meet him down here? There must be some mistake. You're not allowed here."

"Okay. Tell him I stopped by, will you?"

Don't go, don't go! Rory pleaded as he wiggled his fingers through the grating, all the while fighting a pressing urge to jump up and run. *I'm almost there.* Just as he pushed a finger through, the ship lurched and Lucy shifted her feet. *Missed!* He clamped his jaw shut, riding out the cramps in his legs. They felt like a charley horse.

"I'm kinda lost, though," Lucy was saying. "Could you point me to the elevators, or something? I've been sloshing around here, like, forever."

Fishlips groaned irritably. He started to give her directions.

Rory could feel all his muscles tensing, longing to spring. His whole body felt like a rubber band stretched to the limit and ready to snap. He had to hurry.

He forced his fingers up a few holes and poked them through the grating again. He jabbed several times into the sole of Lucy's shoe. *She must feel that!* She moved again, but didn't look down. *Rats. Come on, Lucy, look down!*

"Let me get this straight. Down that way and then hang a lefty. Right?" she was saying.

"No. Turn right."

"Right, right. Thanks large. Sorry to bother you."

Breathing unevenly through his nose, his teeth set so tight his jaw ached, Rory managed to get his fingers back through the grate to poke her foot again. This time she lifted it up and rubbed the sole of her sneaker. She looked down. *About time!* Rory grinned helplessly at her.

"*Uh,* on second thought," she looked back up at Fishlips, "I'm real ditsy with directions. Could you maybe show me the way? I'm real sorry to be such a pest."

"Stupid child!" Fishlips barked and led her away. "You're wasting my time."

Good old Luce! Rory groaned as he rolled out from under the grate. It felt wonderful. Like sitting down after a day on your feet. But, without asking his permission, his legs jumped up and charged off again. He didn't have strength to argue, even if he knew they were taking him to his doom.

He ran across to the far side of the deck, then aft towards the stairs. Stumbling with every shake of the ship, he wound his way around, hardly caring if he was seen.

Crewmen were hustling to deal with the storm. He ducked past them and screeched to a stop when he reached the stairs. Fishlips was right there! He was talking on an intercom with his back to Rory. But Rory couldn't wait. His muscles ached to move.

He snatched a lungful of air and bolted right past. Up the stairs, two and three at a time. Slowing long enough to catch his breath, he looked back. No one was after him.

"Going my way, sailor?" said a voice.

"Lucy!" he cried. There she stood, a couple of steps above him. "Am I glad to see you. Come on!" His legs took over and he ran past her and up the stairs.

"Slow down," she called. "Where are we going so fast?"

They surfaced on Deck 11 and made for the main stairs. Four more decks to go.

The storm got uglier. The one he and Lucy had braved out on the foredeck earlier in the week was like lapping ripples compared to this. The ship was rolling like a carnival ride. The halls were completely deserted except for a few crewmen running to batten down the decks. Rory took it as a sign of strength that he didn't feel seasick at all. He had too many other things to worry about.

"Sorry about yesterday," Lucy said, trying to keep up. "I didn't mean to get you in trouble."

He didn't reply. Just kept running. All the same, he was glad she apologized. And glad she'd come to rescue him. "How'd you know where to find me?" he called.

"Your mom called Grams. I guess the storm woke her and she noticed you were M.I.A. I figured it was here or that poop deck you like. So I scoped 'em both."

"Lucky for me."

"Where to this time? I'm ready to drop."

"You'll see," Rory called over his shoulder as he sped up the main stairs and onto Deck 7. This was the moment of truth and he was terrified. Out in the storm was certain death, but if he didn't go out there, the ship would go down. His demon legs were in charge and he hadn't the strength to resist.

The ship pitched so much, they hit walls and had to grab the railings to keep from falling down or sliding on the tilted floors. Things were banging around, followed by loud curses behind the closed doors of the cabins up and down the empty halls.

Suddenly, bells started clanging and a loud voice shouted over the intercom. Rory paid no notice. They got to the lifeboat stations before he finally came to a stop. Completely out of breath, he looked through the door windows that led to the boats. He was surprised that no one was there.

A moment later, Lucy caught up. "That's some run," she gasped. She threw herself against the wall. "You hear what they said? This is a real emergency! We should get back to our cabins."

Rory didn't answer. He had to concentrate to keep his legs from running further.

"This is that muster place where we did lifeboat drills, right?" Lucy asked. "Are we abandoning ship?"

"Not yet." All he could see outside was the rain pelting against the doors. "I can't see a thing."

"What are we looking for?"

"Morgan is out there somewhere. I know it." He closed his eyes and suddenly could see the deck outside under the swinging lifeboats and huge waves. He couldn't tell exactly where it was. But his legs could. They carried him across the ship to the row of doors on the opposite side. Lucy groaned, but lurched to her feet to follow him.

"It's like a hurricane, or something," she said. "You know, Rory, I hate to admit it, but I'm real scared."

"I know. Me, too," he said. Visions of huge waves outside didn't help, either. His legs were steering him to a particular door. He put on the brakes with a supreme effort.

"You can't be thinking of going out there?" Lucy said. Then added meekly, "Can you?"

Rory was terrified at the thought of what was through that door and out in the storm. It was his own death. He could feel the cold water swallow him up and drag him down, deeper than hell itself, while he clawed frantically for light, air, a chance. At the same time he realized that the only way to save the ship, to save his mom, Lucy, and even Eddie, was to risk it all and find Morgan. He had to face this fear. For Ian, if no one else. He could see right through Lucy's tough exterior. She was scared to death. She'd come this far, but she could go no further. It was up to him and he couldn't afford to hesitate. Not this time.

Without another thought, he crammed his glasses tight on his nose and pushed through the door.

"Rory!" Lucy shouted, and ran up. "Don't! You'll be killed!" She was too late. He was gone.

Outside, the pelting rain and wind brought him into the full face of the gale, knocked him right off his feet, and smacked him into the rail. Under a gray-black sky, waves rising higher than the ship itself rolled in and lifted her up the side of a mountain of swirling dark water, only to crash her down on the other side. Each wave slamming over the deck dumped a shock of cold water over Rory's head. Soaked to the bone and clinging to the tilting rail, slowly, slowly, he worked his way along. She yawed and pitched, like a top on its last spin.

"Morgan!" he shouted. "Where are you?"

Lightning flashed. A thunderclap roared overhead. Another huge wall of water picked him off the deck and flung him into a bulkhead. It was only then that he really understood the danger he was in.

He lurched forward and caught hold of a rail. Another monstrous wave swept the deck and nearly took him with it. But he held tight. The ship started to climb the next summit of water. He felt the deck rise up and leave him swinging helplessly on the railing. All he could do was cling, his legs practically dangling.

"Rory!" Lucy shouted from the doorway. "This is crazy. Come back!" Even though she was still mostly inside, she was drenched. And terrified.

"I can't," he yelled back, and wrapped himself tighter around the rail. In a flash, she was gone. He was alone. More alone than he ever could have imagined.

Wave after wave washed over him. He could feel his hands begin to slip. His glasses flew off in the wind and disappeared. He didn't think he could hold on much longer.

A figure appeared. It was somewhere in front of him on the deck. He could faintly see it hugging the rail. It had its back to Rory and was moving slowly away as Rory called out and tried to catch up. The figure didn't stop, even though he called and called. Without his glasses the figure was just a blur, but Rory knew it was Morgan.

Just as he came up close behind, the hair on his neck pricked up. Something was wrong. He reached out an arm and so did the man. *It's me!*

"Right behind you!" the voice cried. He had been watching himself through the demon's eyes!

Rory screamed and spun around. The fiend in Morgan's body was only a couple of feet away, clawing its way along the deck towards him, a murderous gleam in its eye. He could feel the hate rise off it like steam. Feeding out a coil of rope slung over its shoulder, the demon inched closer and closer, tying it off wherever it could. Rory clung to the rail as the demon stretched out its bony arm to the limit, fingers wriggling to grasp Rory's sleeve. *One more step and he'll have me.* The next battering of icy cold water pounded him against the wind and he lost his grip. He was carried down the deck. Just in time he managed to grab the rail before he was taken overboard.

The demon shrieked with disappointment and followed him as quickly as it could. "Reach out your arm!" it demanded, as it closed the gap between them. "What choice have you?"

I do have to kill him. The thought disgusted him. Hand over bruised hand, Rory crawled down the railings, like climbing rungs on a ladder, to keep from the demon's claws.

"You'll have to trust me. There is no other way," the demon crowed before the next shock of water filled its mouth, choking its words and loosening its grip on the rail. It stretched its arm out again. "Or is there?" it cackled. A flash of lightning lit their faces. Rory saw the demon's maniacal features draw tight with pain and malice.

Rory slumped down on the deck and wrapped himself tightly around a pole. He had no more strength. He was cut and bruised and out of breath. This would be his last stand. Another tower of seawater came at them. It wrenched the creature's hands from the rail and flung it down the deck. It slid several feet on a wash of water. But the rope around its middle held. As it snapped tight around its belly, the demon cried out hideously. For a moment, it lay still. Rory wondered if it had killed him. Then it stirred, looked up, and began again to laboriously pull its way towards Rory.

"Now reach for me! We haven't time. I don't have much strength left." It was Morgan's voice. "For the moment, I have the beast under control, but not for long."

Rory was consumed by fear. "How do I know you won't kill me?" he shouted over the wind. *Kill him first,* insisted the voice in his head. *He's old and weak. No one will ever know.*

"Don't be a fool, Rory! I want to save you."

What do I do? How do I know which one this is? Will he save me or hurl me into the sea? He couldn't hold on much longer, whatever Morgan might do. He had to trust it was Morgan talking to him. He reached out a hand. He felt Morgan's iron grip grasp his hand like a lifeline.

"Let go of the rail with your other arm. I'll pull you to me."

Rory hesitated. His terror was greater than the storm.

"I won't let you go, son," Morgan croaked, spitting water. "I owe it to the other boy as much as to you. I know you're no demon. It's possessing me."

Rory crept towards him while the ship was lifted up and hurled down into the swirling torrent. At the last step, the floor seemed to drop away and he started to slide.

Morgan threw his other arm around Rory and together they rode down a waterslide towards the port side gunwale. The rope cracked tight and Morgan cried out in pain as his arms were yanked back. But he didn't let Rory go.

"Climb over me and take hold of the rope!" Morgan commanded. "I'll be killed if I have to take another jolt like that. Be quick! Before the demon returns."

In the lull, Rory dragged himself over the old man towards the rope. Morgan started to untie it from his own waist to fasten it around Rory. *Now is our chance,* the voice urged. *Save yourself. Push him over. No one will know it was you! When he's gone, I'll make the storm stop!*

That stopped Rory cold. He knew the demon could stop the storm. All he had to do was turn his back on Morgan and let the waves do the rest. *Why not let the demon help me?* It would end this terror, maybe even save his family. In a split second, he made his decision.

"NO, I CAN'T," he screamed at the voice. "Morgan is my friend."

Morgan looked up as he finished the knot around Rory's waist. "You're my friend, too," he said, and then a change spread over his face. The demon's sinister gleam was back. Quick as a rattlesnake strike, it grabbed Rory by the throat with a squeal of delight.

"I have you now, little worm, and you won't get away this time!" the demon snarled, his cold fingers once again squeezing the life from the boy. Rory was so frightened, sore, and tired, he couldn't put up a fight.

The ship leapt out of the sea and sent them sliding back out of control. The demon lost its grip and clawed the air. Rory made a grab for its sleeve, arm, anything! He missed. With horror, he watched the old man get dragged overboard by a wave higher than the railing.

"MORGAN!" he wailed.

Over the roar of the storm he heard a single blood-curdling shriek, like the last cry of an animal meeting a horrible death.

He was yanked to the limit of the rope. The snap felt as if it were ripping his guts out, then jerked him back again. Gasping for air and shivering with cold, he clung tight. He could feel hot tears on his cheeks despite the freezing rain and waves.

Arm over arm, he tried to pull his way along the rope. But his strength was spent. Another crash of water picked him up and heaved him back towards the gunwale. The rope stopped him, but it almost cut him in two.

He bounced from railing to pole and straight over the side, his numb fingers scrabbling at anything to slow himself down. He was about to pitch into the ocean, but the rope held. Hanging over the edge of darkness, he prayed it would hold long enough for the storm to pass.

Another biting cold wave slammed him into the hard steel hull. He hit his head. He could feel his arms go limp. All he could think was that he wanted to see his mother one last time.

As the ship slid back down the trough, Rory felt as though hands were grabbing and pulling him under the water. A loud bang ended the wind and rain. All he could feel was the rocking motion of the sea as the world become both gentle and distant. A vision of his mother's face hung over him.

Then everything went dark.

16

The Curse Is Broken

When Rory opened his eyes, the world was white and quiet. *Am I in heaven?* he wondered. He turned his head and saw his mother dozing in a chair beside his bed. They were in a small white room, with a chair on either side of the bed and all sorts of medical machines at Rory's elbow. His eye followed along the tube that ran from a sack of fluid on a stand into his hand. *I'm on an IV, just like in the movies. I can't be dead.* He looked again at his mom. Her clothes were rumpled and slept in and she looked really pale.

"Mom?" He tried to speak, but his voice sounded like a frog and was painful. Sitting up made him dizzy, so he lay down again.

Claire smiled. "You're awake," she said tenderly, and moved close to kiss him.

"Where am I?" He fumbled around for his glasses and then remembered they were lost in the storm.

"In the ship's infirmary," she explained, and stroked his brow. "You've been in a fever for a day and a half."

"Really?" He tried to sit up again, but a sharp pain in his chest told him to stop. He winced and fell back.

"You broke two ribs and got a concussion," she told him, and fussed with his blankets. "We made an emergency stop in Halifax. We're going to stay here for a day while they fix the damage from the storm."

They looked at each other for an awkward moment. Finally, Claire burst out, "Rory, what were you thinking to go out there like that?"

Rory gulped.

"I mean, it's a miracle that you weren't killed! You disappeared from the cabin in the middle of the night and –" She stopped. Something in Rory's look brought her to a halt.

"Mom, I'm so sorry for everything," Rory croaked, with tears in his eyes.

"Everything is okay. Save your strength. We can talk about this later," she said, more softly. Then she continued after a pause, "Anyway, you were right. I've been so wrapped up in myself since. . . ." She cried and her voice cracked. "I don't want to lose you, too." She pressed her forehead to his. It felt very good.

"Is it too late to make up?" he asked.

"It's never too late for that," she assured him, wiping her eyes. He felt his own warm tears on his cheeks. It had been a long time since that had happened in front of his mom. It made him feel that everything would be alright. "We'll spend more time together, just you and me. We'll get to know each other all over," she said soothingly.

A huge weight lifted. For the first time he thought it wasn't possible for him to control or be responsible for everything.

The nurse marched in, her crisp white uniform practically wearing her. "Awake again? That's good. I bet you're hungry this time." It sounded like an order. She checked his chart, took readings, and examined him like he was some crash test dummy.

He nodded. "What's for grub?"

"I'll see what I can find." She marched back out.

"Captain Ahab!" laughed a familiar voice.

"Lucy!" Rory said as affectionately as his groggy voice could.

"Thought I heard your voice. You made it! How're you feeling?"

"Pretty good for being strapped to a whale." He grinned. She grinned back.

"If Lucy hadn't come and gotten us, we never would have known where you were," Claire said.

She didn't let me down? "Thank you," he choked out.

Lucy pretended to make nothing of it. "You're the hero. The storm stopped in a zap right after you were rescued, like that!" She snapped her fingers. "Grams heard the captain say it was some kind of miracle. He'd never seen anything like it. One minute everybody was dodging furniture and the next, the sun was out."

"That's right," Claire added. "The captain said that the storm was a freak of nature."

A chill ran up Rory's back. He looked cautiously at his mother and then at Lucy. Claire caught the look and got up.

"I'll let you two conspirators talk. But make it quick because I'm coming right back to make sure you eat and get more sleep." She kissed her son and left.

"Guess what I found out?" Lucy began. "It's like he was never here. The captain asked all about him. I showed them your computer, but it got kind of messed up in the storm. They're going to investigate. Probably want to talk to you, too." She looked around at the door. "Where'd he go?" she whispered.

A lump rose in Rory's throat. "He went overboard saving me."

"What!?"

She helped Rory prop himself up on his pillows and he told her everything he could remember. His voice sounded like a coffee grinder, but that didn't stop him.

"You are some cool dude, Ror," said Lucy, when he finished. "I'm so sorry I bailed on you. I've never been so scared in my life. I ran for help."

"Thanks," he said again. He knew that everyone on the ship owed the old man their life. He had sacrificed himself to save Rory and the ship, even while he was struggling to control the demon that possessed him. *That must have broken the curse.* "I was the stupid one for running out there in the first place."

She looked sheepish. "You've got to forgive me for lying to Grams and leaving you swinging the other day, too. I should have backed you up. I just seized."

That wound still hurt. "You shouldn't have done that. I trusted you."

"I know. I'm real sorry. If you'll still be friends, I'll watch your back from now on. Promise. Hanging with you has been better than anything I've ever done in my life."

Rory turned bright red. That was the nicest compliment he'd ever gotten. He didn't know what to think. "Can I be part of your posse?" he asked, before he had time to reconsider.

"You got it! The gang'll be thrilled to have you ride with us when you come to visit."

They sealed it with a handshake as Claire came back with the nurse and a hot lunch for all of them.

The last day of the voyage to New York was peaceful. Rory stayed in bed. Along with the broken ribs and concussion, he had a few stitches, bruises, and a chill that the doctor wanted to make sure didn't turn into pneumonia. He didn't mind being stuck there since he hurt all over and didn't have his glasses. Mom and Eddie spent the day with him and they got to know Lucy and Grams better. They all played games and laughed together. Rory hadn't seen his mom so sunny in years. For her sake, he and Eddie tried to get along better. He even sent Lucy out to buy Eddie a souvenir *Sea Lion* watch, which Eddie said he'd never take off.

Captain Levesque held a preliminary investigation into the disappearance of Morgan Hewett. He took statements from everyone who talked to him and was especially interested in Rory's story. There didn't seem to be any trace of the old man left on the ship, except in the memory of those who had seen him. The captain did admit that there had been a problem with the stabilizers all along, but couldn't understand how Morgan would know anything about it.

Rory couldn't open his computer files. As Lucy had said, the laptop had been tossed around his stateroom so many times in the storm that it sounded like a box full of puzzle pieces. So he went on-line at the Cyber Café to find the original pictures and information on Morgan Hewett. When he found the picture of Mr. and Mrs. Edward Lowrey, he discovered a very strange thing. The Lowreys were the same but there was only one person in the background: the unidentified woman. Morgan Hewett was missing!

Rory quickly searched for the bio page on the Hewetts. Something had changed there, too. The pictures and history were still the same, but it stated that Morgan Hewett had died on the *Titanic* and his wife, Olivia, had been rescued. She died in 1916 of pneumonia!

Rory was convinced that Morgan didn't know most of the time when he was possessed by the demon. He really believed he was making it safer on all the ships, not leading them to their destruction. Rory had felt the fiend firsthand, working its fear inside of him, making him perform tasks he couldn't control. As far as he was concerned, Morgan Hewett had paid for what he did on the *Titanic*.

He thought about the demon trying to get him to kill Morgan so that he would commit an evil act, and wondered if that was how Morgan had been convinced to do it in the first place on the *Titanic*.

Is there some immortal sea demon that goes through history, passing from one tortured sailor to another, preying on their fears and using their own hands to commit terrible deeds? Is that how ships are lost at sea? Is there really such a thing as a mariner's curse?

He hoped he would never find out.

When they finally docked in New York City, Rory was in a wheelchair in Lucy's cabin, listening to her arguing with Grams. "It's not fair that I can't go to Wichita with Rory for the rest of vacation!" she complained. "You're a real Cruella!"

"Oh, do be still, Lucille." Grams was exasperated. "You and Rory will be able to write and we'll plan a visit next summer. Now, leave me alone and don't spoil your good-byes."

Lucy pouted and Rory beamed. He liked to feel that he was going to be missed. He didn't think that had ever happened to him before. He was sad that they were parting, but it was unavoidable.

"We can E-mail," he suggested. "Even instant message and stuff. It'll be great."

Lucy refused to be cheered up. "We don't have a computer."

"We'll get you one," Grams grumbled from the sundeck. "Now stop this nonsense and go spend your last few minutes together. Somewhere else!"

Lucy wheeled Rory to the main lobby. The place was buzzing, like it was a week earlier during boarding. Without his glasses, all the faces were blurry and the furniture was reduced to shapes and shadows. With butterflies in his stomach, he and Lucy hugged and it felt like he could hardly breathe. It wasn't easy saying good-bye.

"We will always be friends," she whispered in his ear.

"I'll hold you to that," he replied, feeling tears well up. Whatever else he was unsure of being true on this trip, his friendship with Lucy was real.

Claire, Eddie, and Grams appeared behind them.

"Are you ready to go, sport . . . I mean . . . Rory?" Eddie asked.

"Sport is okay," he said with a smile, as his mom pushed the wheelchair towards the gangway.

"Mr. Dugan!"

His wheelchair stopped and they all turned.

"Hello, Captain Levesque," said Claire.

Rory squinted to get a clear picture. The best he could make out was the white uniform, two eyes and a mouth in a round pink blotch. "Yes, sir?" he said.

"We found these snagged on one of the lifeboats. They must be yours." He reached out and gave Rory a pair of glasses.

"Thank you," Rory said, accepting them. "What a relief; now I can see." He put them on. Things were blurrier than before. He felt a bit dizzy. Taking them off, he stared at what was in his hands.

They were the old man's spectacles.

The End